Praise for
Echoes and Embers

"*Echoes and Embers* is filled with transmissions from both the future and the past, stories that are tender, beautifully strange, ancestral, cosmic, adventurous, yet mixed with the horrific and the folkloric in settings both familiar and far reaching into space—perfect for readers who want to be both transported yet grounded." —Ai Jiang, Nebula and Bram Stoker Award-winning author of *Linghun*

"Magic. Murder. Mayhem. In *Echoes and Embers*, Pedro Iniguez invites readers into a hauntingly beautiful series of tales imbued with a deep love of Mexican culture. These stories range from the mystical to the macabre. With the unexpected twists of *Black Mirror* and the detailed world-building of science fiction classics, readers of all genres will find much to love. A must read. Five stars!" —D.K. Stone, author of *Inescapable: A Ghost Story*, and the Waterton Trilogy

"*Echoes and Embers* is a compelling collection of stories that showcase great emotional range and extreme depth. At times gentle, brutal, hilarious, heartbreaking, and delightful. Pedro Iniguez spins real magic here!" —Jonathan Maberry, *New York Times* bestselling author of *Burn to Shine* and *Necrotek*

"With a selection of stories from one of the most talented multi-genre writers working today, *Echoes and Embers* lends a unique voice to speculative fiction. Iniguez skillfully subverts tropes and often blends genres, taking the reader on a tour filled with magic, alien worlds, and eldritch horrors, to name a few. Many of the stories take inspiration from the author's Mexican heritage, but even when they don't, the reader can be assured they always have something profound to say." — P.A. Cornell, Nebula finalist author of "Once Upon a Time at The Oakmont"

"*Echoes and Embers* is a collection that shows Pedro's staggering range as a SFF writer. You'll find a little bit of everything in the book, and you'll love all parts of it. Echoes and Embers is the kind of collection that makes you hope Pedro is writing more stories for us right now!" —Renan Bernardo, Nebula and Ignyte finalist author of *Disgraced Return of the Kap's Needle*

"From generation ships to alien planets to dystopian dreamscapes, Pedro Iniguez's storytelling weaves from world to world on a glimmering thread of emotion. In turns visceral and surreal, this genre-hopping collection takes readers on a fantastical, imaginative adventure." —Ren Hutchings, author of *Under Fortunate Stars* and *The Legend Liminal*

"Wonder and terror are present, along with grief and grace. Wide-ranging in tone and subject, these stories are linked by a common thread of melancholy: for what might be, for what might have been. It all makes for an engaging read." —Khan Wong, author of *The Circus Infinite*

"Pedro Iniguez writes himself true in *Echoes and Embers*, to telegraph dreams, murmurs and regrets in unassuming stories enshrouded with ghosts, star falls and space ways. As the ravishing song of the mythical kipi-kua creature flames the atomic embers of hope, new chances and transcendence, distantly familiar characters reposit themselves into intimate lives we get to spend time with in the arresting *paso doble* of Latino-infused text." —Eugen Bacon, British Fantasy Award winner and Philip K. Dick Award finalist

"In tales that are as likely to touch your heart as they are to dazzle or horrify, Pedro Iniguez displays his storytelling prowess and passion for crafting worlds that are anchored to characters that feel deeply real and painfully human." —E.G. Condé, International Latino Book Award winner, Ignyte Award finalist, and Indie Ink Award finalist author of *Sordidez*
"With *Echoes and Embers,* Pedro Íñiguez cements his place as one of the leading writers of Mexican American futurism." —David Bowles,

award-winning author of *The Witch Owl Parliament* and *The Prince & the Coyote*

Also by Pedro Iniguez

Control Theory

Synthetic Dawns & Crimson Dusks

Mexicans on the Moon: Speculative Poetry from a Possible Future

Fever Dreams of a Parasite

The Fib (coming soon)

Echoes and Embers
Speculative Stories

Pedro Iniguez

ISBN: 979-8-9914419-1-9 (hardcover)
ISBN: 979-8-9907055-9-3 (trade paper)
ISBN: 979-8-9914419-0-2 (ebook: ePub)
Library of Congress Control Number: 2025931550

First printing edition: July 15, 2025
Published by Stars and Sabers Publishing in the United States of America.
Cover Artwork: Raúl Cruz | Cover Design and Layout: Dash Creative
Edited by Jendia Gammon and Gareth L. Powell
Proofreading and Interior Layout by Scarlett R. Algee

https://www.starsandsabers.com/

For the dreamers who look to the stars and feel magic in their hearts.

Table of Contents

Echoes and Embers
Speculative Stories

Magic Lucha

"It's like magic," Abuela said, waving her hand across the powder blue sky. "The cheers of the crowd, the electricity in the air. Anything can happen. Can you see it?"

An entire world came alive in Julio's mind. Masked heroes tangled with their nefarious counterparts inside a giant ring as the crowd roared and blue flashbulbs popped off like fireflies in the stands. A wave of elation rippled through his body and for a moment he could've sworn he even felt it surge in his legs.

It had been two years since the car crash took both his parents and his Abuelo. Julio lost his ability to walk, leaving him only his Abuela— who hadn't been in the car—grief, and memories.

Some, though, were very special memories. Those were the ones that still made him smile. Since he was a little boy, for instance, his Abuelo had enchanted him with tales of lucha libre: the mythical clashes, the gravity-defying stunts, the larger-than-life characters. Sometimes stories like that had been enough for a ten-year old boy like him.

He was suddenly conscious of the sun stinging his face again, the heat evaporating his daydreams into the ether. He wicked the sweat from his head and turned to Abuela. She had been doing her best to keep his spirits up while helping him maneuver his wheelchair over the dusty road leading into Oaxaca City. While he usually propelled himself, the rough terrain made it difficult for him to manage without help.

They'd trekked past the foothills of the Sierra Madre Mountains and down into the verdant Central Valley, and every minute that brought them closer to the city made Julio's heart thump a little faster. The excitement over his first lucha libre match was something he found difficult to contain. Abuelo had talked about his love for wrestling as long as Julio could remember. The athleticism, the spectacle of good versus evil, the crowds cheering alongside you. Julio had pictured it all his life. He'd even staged fake matches with the neighborhood kids before the car accident.

His mind wandered again, as it always did, to thoughts about his parents. About Abuelo. His legs. Sometimes he'd have trouble processing that it really even happened at all. He also couldn't help but feel sorry for Abuela, old as she was, pushing him along in the August heat. But it didn't matter to her. She would just shake her head and tell him everything was all right. To her, the destination made everything worthwhile.

"I think I see Oaxaca," Julio said, shielding his face from the sun as he gazed ahead. "How much longer until we get there, Abuela?"

"Not much more," she said, squinting. In the distance, the mangled outlines of cathedrals and radio towers loomed like giant sentinels in the hot air. "The arena is on the fringes of Ndua."

Ndua was the old Zapotec city that became Oaxaca. A world of brave warriors and sage priests. A wondrous place that must have been, Julio thought. Sadly, those times were long gone.

***

Abuela stopped to readjust the tote bag slung over her shoulder, making sure her lilies didn't spill out onto the road.

Occasionally, they'd come upon fellow travelers and Abuela would ask if they were interested in purchasing a lily for a loved one, or perhaps a bendición, a blessing. Some would politely decline. Others would look away while keeping their distance, as if she were contaminated.

"Why do they avoid you like that, Abuela?"

"Because they think I am a bruja, mijo." She smiled, the sunlight beaming off the twin silver braids draping over her shoulders and down her long, embroidered blouse. Her smile gave way to a laugh and the turquoise-beaded necklace around her chest clacked like marbles. "I should be flying us into the city on a broom. Or perhaps I should turn us into bats."

"*Are* you a bruja, Abuela?"

Abuela stifled her giggle with one hand and wiped the slivers of moisture from her eyes with the other. She then wagged a long, wrinkled finger. "No, Julio, our family descends from a long line of Zapotec healers and mystics. These days, though, people aren't keen on the distinction between healer and witch. Take my flowers, for instance. They are meant for healing, not for cursing."

Julio eyed her bag, the white lilies like stars atop green stems. "What's so special about lilies?"

Abuela gazed into the distance as she plumbed the depths of her mind. "Back in the old days, the Zapotecs and the Mixtecs that used to live in this valley were at constant war. One day the Mixtecs captured the beloved Zapotec princess Donají to ensure that peace would be upheld between both nations. But the Zapotecs attempted to rescue their princess, and in an act of vengeance, the Mixtecs slayed their captive and buried her where no one would find her."

"I don't get what this has to do with flowers," Julio said.

"I'm getting there, mijo," Abuela said. "Many years later, a shepherd boy walking near the Atoyac River found a single lily sprouting from the ground. The exotic flower— which was not known to grow in the region— had grown from the buried remains of the princess."

Julio shook his head. "I still don't understand."

"You see," Abuela said, "sometimes something beautiful can grow from the remains of something tragic. That's what the lily represents. Hope. New beginnings. Rebirth. Magic."

Julio thought about the wreath of lilies Abuela had left at the side of the road where the car had crashed. Flowers were nice, but he'd much rather have his parents and Abuelo back.

After some time, the dirt road gave way to the cobblestone streets of Oaxaca. A hodgepodge of cathedrals, markets, and colonial dwellings made up the eclectic veneer of the city. Julio had only been here a handful of times on trips with Abuelo to pick up supplies for his pottery shop.

When Julio saw it, he smiled. Arena Donají jutted from the earth like an ancient coliseum, its dusty, cracked walls showing the effects of solar and wind-whipped erosion. Abuelo would drone on about the small open-air venue and how it had housed many sporting events over its long history. Though he had lamented that the venue had long lost most of its business to modern stadiums, it still hosted the occasional circus act or boxing match, which had made him happy. Anything to keep the place alive.

"Your Abuelo used to come here as a boy and watch every lucha match his parents could afford to bring him to," Abuela said, meeting his gaze. "Then, when we met, he'd take me along with him. We'd bring your father as a boy as well. I wish they were with us now."

Julio thought of the lily wreath at the crash site again, feeling a tug at his heart. He wanted the same thing. Today more than ever. "Can't you bring them back?"

Abuela arched an eyebrow. "What makes you think I could do that?"

"Well, don't you practice magic?" he said with a hint of frustration in his voice.

Abuela pressed her lips into a frown and ran a gentle hand through his hair. "No magic can bring back the departed. Even if I could, fate is not something that can be tamed like a horse or altered like a garment. Like I said, I'm not a witch, mijo. I'm a curandera."

Julio looked at his legs. He wanted nothing so much as to be able to backflip off his fence and onto a table in the backyard, his parents watching, cheering. As a surge of irritation riled up inside, he wondered what a curandera *could* heal; what the scope of their powers was, exactly. Clearly resurrections and miracles were out of the question.

Abuela began to help Julio toward the arena, but Julio put up a hand and said, "Thank you, Abuela, but I can take it from here." She smiled and paid at the small box office as Julio followed her into the arena. The walls were plastered with the peeling posters of luchadores as they kept watch over the spectators rushing to their seats. They were wrestlers he'd never heard of: El Diablo. El Monstruo. El Caballero Bravo.

"These men used to be celebrities," Abuela said. "This country used to revere the sport, and families would flock to every match. Now, the wrestling organizations scrape by with small traveling shows in any town that will host them."

"Who's this one?" Julio said, pointing to the portrait of a wrestler at the end of the hall. His turquoise mask had black trim and small red rhinestones dotting the cutouts around his nose, eyes, and mouth. His muscular arms were crossed around his chest in a pose reminiscent of a comic book superhero.

"Oh," Abuela said, smiling, "that's El Rayo Místico." There was a sense of pride in her voice; of a forgotten joy recaptured. "He was a national hero about twenty years ago. He stopped wrestling and faded from public life when he accidentally ran over a little boy in Mexico City."

Julio gasped. "What happened to him?"

"No one really knows," Abuela said as they made their way through the stands. There, a group of spectators hovered around a tall, slender man in sunglasses. His guitar case was littered with crumpled pesos and betting slips.

"Is that man taking bets?" Julio asked.

"Ignore him, mijo. Best to leave games of chance alone."

Inside, the undercard was underway. Julio had seen their faces up on the walls outside. Mascara Diabolica was battling Chico Atlético. Julio and Abuela took their seats in the upper rows, Julio sitting next to Abuela in an empty wheelchair-accessible space. Together they looked out over the arena. Amidst an ocean of empty orange seats, the few spectators in the arena raised their beers and flailed their arms or waved tiny Mexican flags.

Above, the sun began to sink below the open roof, turning the sky dark blue. A soft breeze rolled in, carrying with it the smell of beer and cinnamon. Of sweat and aftershave. The scents of adulthood. Of Mexico at night.

Inside the ring, the two men traded blows; Mascara Diabolica, the big, brutish heel, walloped the smaller, curly-haired hero into the ropes with a string of chest slaps. The crowd whooped and hollered as he side-kicked Chico Atlético in the chest, sending him tumbling to the canvas with a resounding thud. Before Mascara could pin his opponent, a faint red glow flickered on a dark amulet around Chico's neck just before he rolled out of the way. He sprang up on his feet and clotheslined the bigger man onto the floor. Chico pounced on Mascara Diabolica and pinned him. The referee gave a quick three-count and Chico Atlético claimed the upset victory.

The crowd jeered and booed, some of the fans pulling at their hair.

Julio gawked in awe as he leaned forward in his wheelchair. "No way!"

"It appears people lost a lot of money on this bout," Abuela said.

"Mascara Diabolica had this match won," Julio said, throwing up his arms. "How did Chico Atlético get up so quickly? And did you see that light glowing from his necklace? Like you said, Abuela, it's like magic!"

"Something is different," she said, scanning the crowd. "Something is wrong." Her eyes narrowed on the bleachers on the opposite side of the arena. "I see someone I have not seen in many years. Someone not entirely pleasant."

"Who is it?"

"Doña Mirela Maldonado," she said scowling. "A witch with bad intentions."

"A witch?" Julio followed her gaze until he spotted an old woman draped in a black shawl. The woman threw her head back and appeared to cackle when the man with the sunglasses approached her seat and handed her a handful of cash. She stuffed the money into a fanny pack and rubbed a shiny black pendant hanging around her neck.

"She was banished from the pueblo many years ago for practicing unconventional medicine and magic." Abuela's tone became grave, serious. "Something some of us healers call Blood Magic."

"Blood Magic?"

"It is a wicked, nasty sort of magic. It involves harmful spells, potions, and trinkets used for personal gain or to inflict harm on others." She turned to Julio. "She tried to pry your grandfather away from me using its twisted power. Only a warped mind would find gratification in its uses."

The announcer approached the center of the ring. "Damas y caballeros, please put your hands together for the main event of the evening. First, from Guanajuato, the terrible and greatly feared El Malvado!"

A muscular man sporting dark, shoulder length hair, wearing nothing more than boots and a pair of black trunks, charged down a ramp and somersaulted over the ropes, landing onto the ring with a loud thump. He closed his eyes and raised his fists, as if feeding off the energy from the cheering crowd. An obsidian amulet hung around his neck, similar to the one Doña Maldonado and Chico Atlético were wearing. Like some ancient scrawl, his chiseled chest was scarred with odd symbols.

"That amulet. Those marks on his body," Abuela said. "Those are the brands of a bruja. She's controlling some of the luchadores like puppets to rig the matches in her favor."

Julio peered over at Doña Maldonado. She stared intently at the ring, a toothless grin adorning her face.

"And lastly," the announcer said, "this man ranks as among Mexico's greatest champions, here now, in his thrilling return! Please welcome back El Rayo Místico!"

Julio's eyes widened just as the crowd let out a collective gasp. El Rayo walked down the ramp in his signature turquoise mask and trousers. The camera flashes went off as he ducked slowly under the ropes. Rayo waved at his adoring public, his arms flapping like jelly, his tummy jutting out like a loaf of raw dough. The crowd roared. His time away from the ring was showing, but he was still a legend.

"He's back, Abuela!"

Abuela nodded as she peered at Doña Maldonado.

A swell of fans rushed the lanky bet taker, waving handfuls of cash in his face. The Auditorium broke into chants of "Rayo! Rayo! Rayo!"

The bell rang and the luchadores squared off, each cautiously circling the other with outstretched hands, their fingers curled like talons. Rayo Místico moved first, his delayed windup telegraphing his punch. The amulet around El Malvado's neck flickered like a burning ember, and the heel sidestepped the blow, countering with a backhanded slap to Rayo's face. *Whack*! The hero staggered back a few paces, recovered, and shoved El Malvado into the ropes. The heel bounced off the ropes like a rubber band and sprang forward. He clutched Rayo's neck, lifted him up off the floor, and slammed him down.

Julio winced at the sound of Rayo's body slamming onto the canvas.

Rayo looked dazed, crawling on his belly like an infant. He reached for the turnbuckle and pulled himself up. El Malvado bounced himself off the ropes again and sprinted into a leaping kick which landed square on Rayo's back, sending him flying out of the ring.

The crowd got on its feet, watching as Rayo writhed on the grimy floor. The luchador dragged himself across murky puddles and empty beer bottles, his teeth clenched in pain. Julio could hear his groans from way up where he sat in the nosebleeds.

"Abuela, can't we do something?"

Abuela bit her lip and nodded. "The people have a lot to lose tonight, mijo. Let's see what we can do. Stay put." She patted his head and made her way down the old concrete stairway.

Doña Maldonado shot out of her seat and scowled as she spotted Abuela descending the steps. The witch rubbed her necklace between her thumb and forefinger, a wicked smirk etched across her face. She leaned in and appeared to whisper something into the pendant.

El Malvado's amulet began to flicker like a flame beneath shattered glass. His eyes rolled back into his head and his feet slowly came off the ground until he was levitating over the ring. Arena Donají fell silent; the only sound was the subtle scraping of the wind against its old walls.

Abuela shuffled her way toward Rayo Místico, waving off a pair of confused security guards. She knelt beside the downed hero and placed both hands on his cheeks. She tilted her head against his, closed her eyes, and uttered something Julio couldn't hear. She draped her beaded necklace over his neck and plucked a lily from her bag. She delicately touched the flower to his shoulders, like a queen knighting a squire.

Everyone oohed and ahhed as El Malvado hovered over the ropes and down the ring.

Rayo Místico gazed into Abuela's eyes and nodded. He shot up on his feet and turned toward El Malvado, who was already levitating above him. Both luchadores exchanged a few heated words Julio couldn't make out. Like a supervillain, El Malvado closed his eyes and burst into a fit of laughter. While he was distracted, Rayo hopped up and grabbed Malvado's legs, pulling him to the floor.

Abuela reached under the ring, retrieved a metal folding chair, and tossed it to Rayo, who grabbed it and swung it at El Malvado's head, sending him stumbling backward into the ring. The crowd erupted in a bout of screams and hollers.

Rayo slid under the ropes and raised his arms in the air. The cheering grew louder, electric, just like Julio had pictured it. Everyone in the arena got on their feet.

El Malvado crawled toward the ropes and lifted himself up, his face flush with anger. His amulet flared like a wildfire. The heel balled his hands into fists, his biceps bulging. El Rayo ran up behind him, wrapped his arms around his waist, and suplexed him onto the canvas. El Malvado squirmed on the floor, his mouth spewing a string of vulgarities. El Rayo got back on his feet and dropped, his elbow coming down on Malvado's solar plexus.

The men in the audience removed their hats and waved them in the air. El Rayo yanked on Malvado's pendant, breaking it off his neck. He stomped on the amulet with his boots, shattering the obsidian into a dozen shards.

El Rayo quickly pinned El Malvado into a three-count. The roar of the crowd swelled until it filled the building. El Rayo Místico faced his audience, arms raised in triumph. The crowd rushed into the ring, many tossing lilies at his feet. Children reached out to get a glancing touch of their famed hero. A pair of men hoisted Rayo on their shoulders and paraded him around Arena Donají.

Julio's arms ran electric as the hairs on his skin turned prickly. He felt moisture pooling under his eyes, and for a moment his Abuelo and his parents were sitting beside him, basking in the victory with the crowd.

He turned toward Doña Maldonado. Her seat was empty. The man with the guitar case was swamped with people trying to collect their winnings.

Abuela shuffled back up the steps, the bag of lilies now empty. She stuffed a few crumpled bills into her bag and smiled.

"How did you do it, Abuela?" Julio asked. "Were you controlling El Rayo like Doña Maldonado?"

Abuela shook her head. "I cannot change fate, Julio. I merely convinced him that he was worthy of himself and of the people watching. Sometimes healing begins with believing you are capable of the impossible."

Julio nodded. Her words settled in his heart. Like magic.

"Curandería is really neat," Julio said, looking over the faces of elated fans. Their happiness filled him with happiness. Sometimes, he supposed, feeling hope and joy was the best medicine. In that way, lucha and curandería were not that different. "Could you teach me, Abuela?"

She smiled. "It would be my pleasure, mijo. First, you have to learn how to sow the seeds that will sprout into the most beautiful lilies. Tomorrow, we'll plant some."

Julio nodded. The prospect of tomorrow could not come soon enough.

Together they watched as the people celebrated its hero. Rayo beamed, a joyous look on his face as the crowd carried him outside. Out on the road, as the sun finally sank below the horizon, Julio replayed the entire evening in his head. He couldn't wait to come back another day. Ndua really was a neat place. A place of wonder and possibilities. He smiled, elated that the people had their new champion, and he got to go back home with his.

A Final Song for the Ages

The *Esperanza* was doomed. The generation ship moaned as it tore apart module by module, plate by plate. Nora's father scooped her off the bed and sprang down the corridor. Behind them her mother rummaged through supplies, stuffing what she could inside a large duffel bag. Her mother's screams were drowned out by screeching metal, but Nora thought she said something about a damaged propulsion drive.

Her father entered the escape pod and secured Nora gently inside its stasis chamber. He placed Pepe, her favorite stuffed narwhal, in her hands and smiled. Not long afterward, her mother nestled the duffel bag directly beneath the door and crossed herself, whispering a prayer under her breath.

Her father's fingers zipped across a control panel. The door slid shut, cutting her off from her parents, who each now placed a hand against the pod window. She could make out the words they mouthed. "Te queremos. We love you."

Nora opened her mouth to call out to them, but as always, no words came. A mist enveloped her stasis chamber, drizzling her arms with tiny cold beads of moisture. The droplets seeped inside her lungs. She felt drowsy, her grip on the narwhal slipping as her fingers went numb.

The escape pod rumbled for a moment before it jettisoned into space. Before sleep took her, the behemoth of metal collapsed on itself in a storm of scrap and debris.

But it was a dream. A memory. A regret.

Nora stirred from her sleep and sat up. Groggily, she peered out the pod window. The sky was dark blue. The sun had yet to climb over the mountains on the horizon. Planet Tierra Tres, as it was known back on Mars. Earth Three.

She grabbed her pencil and etched a new tally mark onto the piece of paper pinned on the wall. She did a quick calculation in her head. It was her ninth birthday. Two full solar revolutions on this world. It was a technicality. How many years elapsed as she hurtled through space? Ages, surely. She hugged Pepe and pretended he was two other people at once. She stood, yawned, and opened the hatch. Outside, many Kukumanos were already rousing and scuttling from out of their underground shelters as they prepared for the daily toils of frontier life. She stretched, fixed her mother's straw hat over her head, and prepared to join them.

⌁

Nora stepped out under the shadow of a wooden canopy. Judging from the gathering storm clouds, she was lucky to have one above her escape pod, which had served as her sleeping quarters for the better part of two standard Earth years.

Ahead of her, a series of concrete walkways connected the colony like a grid. Every path led to something: an underground dwelling, a watchtower, an infirmary. Beyond the simple subterranean dwellings stretched a lush, verdant world. Jungles, mountains, raging rivers.

The settlement now stirred with the familiar sounds of scraping legs and clacking mandibles. Before she could make her way toward the colony center to pick up her daily assignment, she heard Krika's unmistakable voice.

"You're on digging duty today," Krika said in her language, hammering her mandibles together in a string of clicks and pauses akin to Morse code from Old Earth. "Rain is coming, and we need at least five dens on the northern end of the colony." Her left mandible was broken at the tip, a memento from a battle with a hungry horned owl long ago.

"*Five?*" Nora protested, snapping her thumb and middle finger in her best mimicry of the Kukumano language. She had no language of her own to offer them on account of a severe laryngeal infection that had left her with paralyzed vocal cords as a toddler. "My hands start to hurt after three."

"Many eggs are expected to hatch within the week," Krika said, the hard clacks of her mandibles suggesting impatience or perhaps anger.

Krika was like the rest of the Kukumanos, having a slender, eight-foot-long body made up of sixteen segments, each bearing a pair of legs. She also had a flat head with a pair of long antennae, sharp mandibles, and two glassy, bulbous eyes.

They were like Earth's centipedes in many ways, except they were sentient and smart. She had read about them on those quiet weeks aboard the *Esperanza*, when her father and the engineering team had been away making repairs while the rest of the settlers remained in stasis.

Krika handed Nora a spade.

"Can I have a word with Okikoa?" Nora pleaded. Her snaps were barely audible, conveying submissiveness. "Maybe I can forage for bugs."

"You know what he'll say," Krika said, scuttling away. "The world beyond the colony is too dangerous. Besides, if you want to be a part of this community, you'll do what you are assigned."

Nora ambled sleepily past the rest of the Kukumanos as they set about digging, hunting, or patrolling the perimeter in search of predators. She found the last den north of the colony and made a mark in the earth about twenty feet away under the shade of a tree. She set down her portable stereo, popped in her mother's favorite CD, and knelt on the dirt as Vicente Fernández crooned *Volver, Volver*.

Some of the Kukumanos stared, agitated at the music blaring from the stereo. Some of the kids on the generation ship were the same way. They'd teased her for playing that *Mexican cactus music*. They didn't understand the words, the melodies, its cleansing effect on the soul. Even at its saddest, it was a celebration of life.

Nora jabbed the small spade into the earth and scooped, closing her eyes and nodding her head slowly, rhythmically. She smiled. She couldn't sing but sometimes the most beautiful things in life simply required listening. And like a temporal wormhole, the music transported her, gifting her, for a brief moment, her mother. Even now she could hear and envision her bellowing out the song as she showered before a shift at the hydroponic garden. It was the happiest her mother had been before a long day at work.

After an hour, Nora had carved out an upside-down dome ten feet deep. Later, someone would come reinforce the insides with mud and finely ground stone. Then another worker would climb the tree and erect a wooden canopy above the dwelling and a new den would be complete.

She stared at the hole. It looked cozy. More than anything, it was practical. The Kukumanos burrowed in order to shelter from predators and the elements. They weren't too unlike humans. Nora found that comforting on most days. They were the closest thing to family she had. Yet even that was never quite enough.

Nora removed her mother's straw hat and wiped the sweat from her face. Or was it tears? On some days she couldn't tell. She sighed and wondered if farm work back on Mars was just as taxing. Or on the *Esperanza*. Her mother would probably say it didn't matter. All that mattered was that at the end of the day, you were alive. And if you could end that day with a smile, you were already winning at life.

Clouds blotted out the late-afternoon sun and rain began to pelt the ground just as she finished digging her fifth hole. She would have to reshape the holes another day when they dried. For now, many of the laborers were already scuttling back into the safety of their dens. She packed her gear and prepared to return to her pod.

"Young one," the voice behind her clacked. "I have news to relay to you." The colony chieftain arched his back so that he was standing to meet her at eye level.

"Hello, Okikoa," Nora snapped her fingers in response. "What is it?"

"Since you came to us two revolutions ago, you have toiled and earned your place beside us, but we have not been honest with you." He turned to face north, his mandibles opening wide for long moment before shutting. Nora had come to associate that with a deep sigh. "On the other side of this jungle lie the bones of a human settlement."

Nora felt her heart drop into her stomach.

"Long ago, an exploratory crew of human engineers built the settlement in anticipation of your ship's arrival. We partook in formal diplomacy, communications, trade. Shortly before you came to us, their numbers had thinned out and ultimately, they perished."

"From what?"

"We believe this planet may harbor some unseen dangers to your people's immune systems. Perhaps toxic water or even deadly spores. Perhaps disease broke out. That is why we tried to keep you safe within our ranks."

Nora swallowed a dry lump.

"Your people constructed a radio tower. It remained dormant, until now. My scouts recently reported hearing a sporadic series of grunts and moans emanating from the tower. We have come to understand it as garbled humanspeak. We do not grasp your technology and have no way of communicating in return. We assume you may be able to contact your species. Perhaps they can arrange for your retrieval."

Nora didn't know how to feel. Her insides knotted up and squirmed simultaneously. She was both eager and sad. She missed people that looked like her, but she had no one to come home to. Where *was* home? Mars had been ravaged by war while countless other settlers departed for faraway worlds. "I would like very much to investigate the radio tower," she replied, snapping her fingers gently, trying hard not to stumble over her words or sound too desperate.

"Tomorrow, you shall travel alongside Ikkak, one of my scouts. Do what you need to do. It will be the only time I allow it."

Drenched, Nora bowed her head as Okikoa scurried away.

On the way back to her pod, she plucked a sweet-smelling orange flower known as the *oolok-kio*. It bore a strong resemblance to an Earth marigold. She tucked it carefully inside her jumpsuit pocket and entered her pod.

Nora retrieved the two portraits she'd drawn that first week she'd arrived on Tierra Tres. It wasn't anything fancy—just crayon on ruled paper—but it was enough to get her through most days. She propped the portraits of Angie and Teodoro Tamayo on a shelf.

Next, she placed the oolok-kio flower between their portraits and lit the candle she'd crafted from tunnel-weasel fat. The flame's light gave their portraits a sense of warmth and life. She ran a finger along their waxy, painted cheeks and smiled through the cascade of warm tears. On some nights she pretended they were staring back at her through loving eyes. Sometimes she came close to believing it. On those nights, her heart ached a little less.

The ofrenda was all she could offer to honor their memory. Her mother had taught her that ofrendas were a way of keeping the dead alive. That their spirits would use the altar as a beacon to the mortal plane in order to visit loved ones. She kept smiling, in the hopes that her parents would see how much joy they brought her.

She crossed herself and uttered a prayer in her head, asking them for things she knew they couldn't give her. Most importantly, she asked for help. For guidance. They hadn't prepared her for a life without them.

Nora blew out the candle, removed her wet clothes, and slid into her cot. Outside, as the sky grew dark, twin ivory moons hovered above the jungle. She hugged Pepe, closed her eyes, and hoped that for once, she'd have a good dream.

～

Ikkak was quiet, but that didn't bother her. She was in awe of the jungle and didn't really feel like talking, anyway. She squeezed Pepe against her chest. It was all so much to take in. Giant ferns, dancing milkweeds, bioluminescent fungi growing under the shadows of colossal trees. The scout had politely and deliberately slowed his crawling pace to accommodate her bipedal debilitation. She was more than sure he'd considered upright walking a handicap.

They traversed north, past the last Kukumano outpost, past the winding creeks, and deep under the thick jungle canopy where sunlight seldom pierced. The air here was suffocating and moist, yet there existed a variety of sweet and musky scents.

Mars never had anything like this. Not even the indoor parks came close. She'd never ventured past the domed cities, but she had known there was nothing there but dust and heaps of rusty-red rocks. She pictured Earth looking much like this, so it didn't surprise her that the *Esperanza*'s crew had chosen this as one of a few possible locations to settle after the Martian Civil War.

She thought about them: the crew of settlers lost to the void of space. What had happened, she wasn't sure. A big explosion. Or was it an implosion? Her father surely would have known. She wished she could ask him.

"What do you carry in your bag?" Ikkak clacked, shaking her from her thoughts.

Nora regarded her backpack. "Gifts my parents left me," she snapped her fingers in reply.

"What kind of gifts did they leave you?"

"Clothes. Books. First aid kits. Portable stereo."

"I don't understand those gifts."

"Things to help me survive."

"Yes, I understand that. Tools."

"Yes," she replied. "They gave me the tools to survive."

After some time, the world grew dark, and her legs felt heavy. "Can we stop to rest?" she asked, snapping her fingers loudly to draw his attention.

"Yes," Ikkak replied. He promptly clambered up a tree and ingested a slew of small insects crawling along the bark.

Nora sat at the base of the same tree and sipped water from a canteen. "How much farther is it?"

"Not far." Ikkak climbed down. His exoskeleton was etched with scars and scratches.

"What are those marks on your body?" Nora asked, snapping her fingers and making a slashing motion in the air.

"Life as a scout is dangerous." Ikkak bent his body back so that he was looking at the jungle canopy.

Nora followed his gaze. Scant patches of sky were visible, but she could see now that it was nighttime from the twinkling of stars. With the darkness came the vibrant sounds of the nocturnal world. All around she heard chirping and buzzing, even growling far off in the distance. She wrapped her arms around her chest and shrank within herself.

Ikkak crawled beside her and rested on the ground at her feet.

A loud, piercing sound made her jolt upright. It was a distinctive screeching not far from where she sat. She leaned forward. It was shrill but almost melodic, with purpose. Like music. She slowed her breathing, hoping to get a better listen.

It came once more, emanating as a series of screeches followed by temporary pauses, only for the screeching to resume again. *Eeeeeh eeh eeeeeh.* Pause. *Eeeeeh eeh eeeeeh.* Pause.

"What is that sound?" Nora asked, quickly snapping her fingers.

"That is the *kipi-kua*," Ikkak replied. "I have not heard its call in many, many revolutions."

"What is a kipi-kua?"

Ikkak pushed off the ground. "I can show you."

They trekked over thin meadows and a few rotting tree stumps toward a small clearing where moonlight shone over reddish soil.

"Do you see it?" Ikkak asked, his clicks hushed in the dark.

A small round head sporting a pointed snout jutted up from under a burrow. The creature pulled itself halfway up by its long-clawed paws.

"I see it," Nora snapped in reply, taking a few steps closer. As she did, she noticed the animal's scaly-plated skin and its milky-white eyes. "It's blind?"

"Yes. They are subterranean, remaining dormant for many cycles. They only surface to eat and mate. This is its mating call. I thought them all gone."

"Why is that?" Nora asked, keeping her eyes on the creature as it jerked in its hole. It was almost pangolin-like, only rounder, stubbier.

"They have not been seen or heard for a long time. Much of their environment was destroyed by your people when they built their colony atop their habitat."

Her face flushed. She felt guilt gnawing at her insides. Like she was going to be sick. Her people caused this?

The kipi-kua's nose prodded the air around it, sniffing insistently for something just like a puppy.

Ikkak continued. "They inhabit a specific portion of land on this planet, preferably near soft, fertile soil. Your people found the area suitable for farming. They plowed over a large swath of kipi-kua territory."

The kipi-kua tilted its head and screeched its melodious song, pausing every so often before continuing.

"Why does it sing and stop like that?"

"It is a song meant for two partners. The gaps in its call are meant to be filled out by another kipi-kua. That is how they find one another. It appears this one sings for a mate that will never come."

A duet, Nora thought. She felt warm tears pool under her eyes. She knew she was crying for both of them. She hoped that there were more of its kind around. For the kipi-kua's sake. For her people's sake.

"Let us continue," Ikkak clacked, "the radio tower is near."

She wiped her tears, and they continued through the jungle until they came upon a slope littered with fragments of bones. She found the strength not to ask. On the other side she saw the sprawl of modules, chain-link fences, even flowing canals as they intersected parts of the colony. All was quiet expect for the sound of small chirping insects.

Ikkak led her toward the western end of the colony. A steel-latticed radio mast shaped like a long triangle had been erected at the crest of a hill. They entered the control room located at its base, which had been left dark and empty. She half expected someone to greet her, but she knew better.

Ikkak turned to guard the door. "Can you initiate contact?"

"I don't know," she said, flicking a light switch. The rumble of generators came to life. To her amazement, the room lit up.

Nora glanced over a series of computers and control panels until she found a microphone jutting out from one of the terminals. A decal of sound waves emanating outward from a radio mast was plastered beside the microphone. She flipped a switch, and a red light blinked on. "Ready for transmission," a synthesized voice spoke.

In the silence of the room the realization came. She balled her small hands into fists and for a long moment she stared at the light. At that moment she felt the urge to scream.

Instead, she sat and slumped her head, slamming a single fist on the counter.

"What is the matter?" Ikkak asked, craning his long neck.

Nora shook her head. "This machine requires audible vocal transmissions. I can't speak in the language of my people," she said, her finger snaps weak, nearly silent. She placed two fingers to her throat. "An old infection messed up my ability to talk. I have no way to communicate."

"Perhaps I could speak for you?"

"No," she snapped in response. "Whoever were to receive the transmission would just hear clacking."

Nora buried her face in her hands. What she would give to have her father hold her, or to hear her mother sing Vicente Fernández one more time.

Her mother's voice echoed in her head, her soothing vocals almost nudging Nora. A wide smile streaked across her face. She unzipped her backpack and probed inside until she found what she was looking for. She flipped the transmission switch on the control panel, grabbed her portable stereo, and thumbed the Play button.

She chose her mother's favorite song, "Volver, Volver." The violins, guitars, and trumpets boomed harmoniously off the speakers as Vicente Fernández crooned about a lost love.

As she nodded her head to the rhythm, she began to snap her fingers, translating so that Ikkak could understand.

"Woeful poetry," Ikkak said.

"Yes," Nora replied, smiling.

Her smile abruptly faded. She began to wonder if the signal would even reach anyone.

Something her father had taught her came back to her just then. While radio waves traveled at the speed of light in a vacuum, those waves eventually became weak and blended in with the background noise of the universe.

She sighed, the sting in her heart deep and piercing. The universe itself was working against her. The music would just become distorted, undecipherable nonsense.

Nora thought of the kipi-kua. Its beautiful song, an exercise in futility. A most wondrous tune meant for someone and no one all the same. They were alike: alone and the last of their kind on Tierra Tres.

She let the song play all the way through. When it was over, she turned off the transmission. She'd offered no coordinates, no clear message. But it was all she could do. She wouldn't be allowed to try again. A final song for the ages, she thought. Like the kipi-kua, her kindred spirit, she was calling out into the void to a people who may never come.

Echoes and Embers

Since she was a girl, Alina Mendez had seen ghosts. They'd appeared in varying states of pain and distress, and though they never lasted longer than a few seconds, the images always bored themselves deep into her conscience.

Anguished screams, contorted faces, grasping hands; she'd seen it all.

Most of the time, in the privacy of her room, she'd press her eyelids shut and curl up into a ball until the moment passed. Unless, of course, she was in public; there, she'd gotten good at turning away, holding her breath, and waiting for them to disappear.

Tonight, she woke to a short, slender apparition—a teenage girl—standing at the edge of her bed, her translucent body nearly blending into the shadows. But tonight, there were no screams. The girl simply closed her eyes, smiled, and wrapped her arms gently around her spectral body. In a flicker of light, the ghost had been torn asunder in a wisp of blue smoke. She was gone before Alina could rip her gaze away and cry.

A surge of blood swelled inside Alina's head. She swallowed a dry lump and tried to sink back into bed. She inhaled a deep breath, letting the cool air settle the fire in her lungs as her heart knocked against her chest. She'd been fortunate; this encounter had been an unusually peaceful one.

Alina wished she knew what had been happening to her. All the CAT scans had come back negative. No brain tumors. No scarring along her brain. She'd never had an emotionally traumatizing experience growing up. Dad had said they were just the souls of those who'd died an untimely death or who'd had unfinished business in the mortal plane. Mom told her they were sinister spirits wandering the Earth looking for innocent people to drag to the underworld and that she should take her rosary and do twenty Hail Marys.

Alina didn't know what she'd seen, but she didn't care for either of those explanations. That couldn't be it.

Her phone rang.

"Hello?"

"Hey," Jamil said. There was a tinge of excitement in her best friend's voice.

"Jamil, it's late," Alina said.

"I know, but there's something I think you'll want to see. I want you to meet me tomorrow. I want to show you something that's gonna change your life."

"Did you happen to hack into Mr. Norton's computer and download the answers to our final exam?"

Jamil chuckled. "Nope. Even better."

"Even better?" Alina said. She stared at the void of darkness where the phantom girl had stood. Occupying the same space was her desk and a pile of dirty laundry. "Ok, Jamil. If it'll get me out of the house for a bit."

* * *

It was always something different. Sometimes the ghosts would be hunched under a chair at school, or pulling out their hair in the middle of the street as their skin flaked away in a storm of ectoplasmic particles. This afternoon, there were two: a man and a girl in pigtails on the corner of Cesar Chavez and Alameda, where Jamil was supposed to meet her. The man, who was dressed in a grey business suit, reached for the child with outstretched arms as she screamed inconsolably. A bike zipped between them, and they were gone.

"Hey," a voice called out. "You ready?"

Alina turned. Jamil flipped his visor behind his head and waved.

"You know I'm not supposed to be down here," she said, looking over the ruins. It had been a while since she'd been down this part of the city. It had always made her feel uneasy. "Besides, we have finals this week and I need to be studying."

"I know, but I think you'll wanna see this."

She smiled. Jamil had been her best friend since middle school, and there was no way he'd have brought her here if it wasn't important.

Behind him, the sprawl of Old Los Angeles greeted her: rusted cell towers, downed powerlines, tattered office buildings, jutting slabs of concrete; all the remnants of an earthquake that had left most of the city in ruins years ago. The only people that still occupied this scrap heap were the destitute, like refugees and squatters, with nowhere else to turn.

Jamil gently interlocked his fingers between hers and led her toward the vestiges of Union Station.

***

The lift rattled and swayed as it descended past rusted beams, cracked pylons, and the rest of the building's old bones. She held her breath and hoped the lift could wither the aftershock.

"They're getting more frequent, aren't they?" Jamil asked.

She nodded, scowling. The fault line had been extremely active the last few months, triggering fears of another major quake across Southern California.

They exited the lift deep in the bowels of Union Station and followed a long, winding access tunnel that led to a wide cavernous space filled with machines, wires, and conductors. Stuff she didn't understand all too well. Here, the air was still and warm. Suffocating, even.

At the tail-end of a snaking line, teenagers stood side-by-side with grizzled adults under the shadows of massive looping pipes. Everyone appeared nervous and fidgety, like they weren't supposed to be there.

"Whatever this is," Alina scowled, "I'm guessing it's illegal."

"It's this new game called *Temporal Reality*," Jamil said, shuffling toward a spot at the back of the line. "After the quake, some engineers tunneled down here and secretly built a particle accelerator. No one knew they'd been digging because people just assumed the tremors from the drills were aftershocks."

"All that radiation," Alina said, looking around. "Aren't particle accelerators dangerous?" She crossed her arms. "Why are we really down here?"

Jamil smiled and shrugged off her question. "The physicists on the project learned they could bombard people with subatomic particles like tachyons, causing their atoms to vibrate at extremely high speeds. This radioactive blast can send a person's molecular footprint back in time. People can go back, explore, learn."

"First," Alina said, "I don't believe you. Second, why did you think I'd be interested in something like this? History is not my strong suit."

They made their way toward the front of the line, where an attendant gauged their sizes and held up two black spandex suits covered in electrodes.

Jamil grinned. "Oh, you'll see."

They stood inside the belly of the accelerator. It was cold and dim inside the metal tubing. There came a loud buzz and Alina squeezed Jamil's hand. Lights flickered manically before darkness filled her world.

In an instant she'd been standing on a swath of golden grass where dandelions swayed in a light breeze. She stood near the lip of a flowing stream, its waters emptying into a river that wound its way along the foothills of a long mountain range. Thatched huts lined the riverbanks where a group of women hunched over small bushes as they gathered berries.

"What the heck is going on?" Alina said, her mouth agape in wonder.

"Tongva," Jamil said as a gust of wind blew through his curly hair. "Native peoples of what would become Los Angeles." He'd been wearing the black skinsuit, except now he appeared translucent, a bluish haze emanating from his body.

"Jamil," Alina gasped, her lips quivering. She brought her hands in front of her face. They were radiant like Jamil's body. "Why are we glowing? We look like-"

"Ghosts?" He smirked. "Our atoms are supercharged and bouncing around erratically. It's like they've become temporal embers. We're basically atomic echoes from the future."

"This... this is why you brought me, isn't it?"

For a moment there was only the sound of the wind rustling through the grass and the rushing of the river's silver waters. A few birds squawked overhead as they circled lush hills.

"I think this may account for those sightings all your life. But not just yours. It takes a lot of energy to douse someone with this kind of radiation. What people have regarded as ghosts through the ages may just have been time travelers. Like us."

"Time travelers." She repeated the words in awe and felt a slight pull at her insides. A feeling of pure joy. Alina hugged Jamil.

Two Tongva women who'd drifted from the tribe spotted them and shrieked. Before long, the entire tribe had gathered along the riverbank, staring at the two specters standing before them. Some of the men began to trot their way. Jamil grabbed Alina's hand and slapped an electrode on his chest.

In a fraction of a second a moment of darkness passed between them, and they were back inside the belly of the accelerator.

Her heart raced. She felt like she'd partaken in some divine miracle not meant for mortal eyes.

Alina turned to Jamil. She didn't know what to say. How could she? It was all so much to take in. Time travel. Subatomic particles. Ghosts. Tongva. Real honest-to-goodness Tongva untainted by colonizer hands. Her head was a tangle of conflicting thoughts. Of impossibilities made real.

"I wanted to show you that there's nothing to be afraid of," Jamil said. "Sometimes the things we fear the most are just things we haven't been able to understand yet."

When her heart finally settled, she nodded and allowed herself to smile.

—∞—

"Thank you again," she said, planting a kiss on his cheek.

Jamil blushed and rubbed the back of his head. "Don't mention it. I hope this eases your mind going into finals."

"Oh, I think it has," she said. "I think everything is going to be alright now. Anyway, I've got to get back home before Mom and Dad kill me."

"I hear that," Jamil said. He turned back toward Old Los Angeles. "See ya at school."

The sun began its descent over the western horizon and if she hurried, she could catch the last bus into New Los Angeles before her parents returned home from work.

A group of construction workers gathered by the bus stop for the last ride into town. Alina leaned against a lamppost and reflected on all the crazy things she'd just experienced. Temporal embers. Echoes from the future. It was almost too much to ingest. But she'd witnessed those things. They were real. Right?

She looked at her hands again. They were fleshy, solid, fully corporeal. How she must've appeared to those Tongva women. The terror they must have felt. Like she had all those years.

She scratched her head as a thought crept into her brain. If the specters she'd seen were time travelers, why did they always seem tormented? In pain? Besides the girl from last night, they were never peaceful encounters.

Suddenly the ground trembled and the lamppost began to sway, its base creaking. Alina stepped back. Windows on skyscrapers burst, hailing crystalline shards on the people below.

The streets fissured open and fire hydrants ruptured, causing white water to cascade down the sidewalks, resembling something out of a biblical flood.

There was a loud boom, and blinding spears of light burst from Union Station's perforated roof.

Alina shielded her eyes with her hands and spun away. There, down the fractured sidewalk, she saw something familiar: a man in a grey business suit reaching for a little girl in pigtails, her screams nearly drowned out by the thunder of the explosion at their backs. A wave of light engulfed father and daughter, fragmenting them into billions of tiny pieces. Like atomic embers.

She wanted to run after Jamil. To hug him.

But it was too late to turn.

The slew of people around her vanished into the ether in trails of bluish vapor.

As the warm light bathed her skin, Alina finally understood. She closed her eyes, smiled, and crossed her arms over her chest in the hopes that some little girl somewhere in the past would never have to fear her final echoes.

And the light swept through the city until there was nothing left to see.

Sierra Starfall and the Elders of the Spaceways

The interceptors, resembling the carapaces of scarab beetles, thrusted through space. The sun glimmered across their frames, illuminating them against the darkness of the void. The patrol ships of planet Hesperia Ultima broke file and fanned out as they pursued the crew of the *Marauder*.

Captain Sierra Starfall gazed out the stern window. She counted four interceptors, shimmering like diamonds in the distance.

"How far now?" she asked, keeping her eyes on the ships.

"We'll enter the asteroid belt in three minutes," First Officer Diablo Caspian said, stroking his long grey beard. "After that they lose jurisdiction to the Prefecture of Beltway Miners."

"They'll reach us before then," replied Helmsman Rags Syntar. His metallic frame swiveled away from the console, turning to Starfall. "They will either board us or shoot us down."

Deckhand Kurt Killborn removed the straps from his seat, stood, and unclasped his pistol. "They blasted our cannons off when we left Hesperia Ultima. We're sitting ducks." Killborn removed a stray strand of blond hair from his face. "Our only chance at a fair fight is if they board us."

Diablo Caspian unsheathed a short, curved cutlass. "We've been here before, Captain," Caspian said, the sparkle of the sword's jeweled hilt matching the fury in his eyes. "We know what to do if they board."

"We wait," she said. "Until they get closer. Killborn—stand by the console and wait for my command. Syntar—keep us on course. Caspian—you can put that sword away."

"What do you have in mind?" Caspian asked.

"We wait until we reach the asteroid belt," she said.

Syntar swiveled back to the helm and nodded. Caspian raised a single eyebrow.

Starfall took a step toward the curved window that wrapped around the ship's stern. She wondered how cold it was out there in the darkness of space, and about how much pain a body could endure as it floated in the vacuum. She felt the warmth of her breath bounce off the glass as the pane frosted over. When she wiped the window, the interceptors had closed the distance on the *Marauder*.

A small sparkle, like a pinwheel firework, launched from the tip of the lead ship.

"Captain," said Caspian, eyeing the command screen, "they have launched a concussion missile."

"I see it. Await my command."

She watched the missile as it approached, marveling at its beauty. It twinkled like the stars in the distance. They reminded her of the countless gems she and the crew had plundered over the years. When they still had luster. When she still cared.

"Captain," said Killborn.

Starfall turned around and gazed through the bow window. The asteroids grew larger by the second.

"Have our escape pods taken any damage?"

"No," Killborn replied.

"Very well." Starfall returned her gaze to the stern. She took the tip of her index finger and drew a smiley face in the frost.

Killborn leaned forward to speak in Caspian's ear. "I know I'm new here," he whispered, "but she's clearly lost it. I say we take over before we're all killed."

Caspian's brow furrowed. "I'd watch what I say, young one. The captain has a wandering mind, but that makes her no less fit to lead. Starfall always has a plan. Now keep your eyes on that console like you were instructed."

Killborn sneered and returned to his console.

Starfall watched as the missile propelled itself through the dark fabric of space, the twinkle growing into a large fiery blaze with a tail like that of a comet.

"We're approaching the first of the asteroids, Captain," said Syntar.

"Killborn," Starfall said, looking at the moisture on her finger, "jettison one of our escape pods. Aim it at the missile. Syntar, fly us behind one of those asteroids. It should confuse their instruments."

"Y-yes, Captain," Killborn said, tapping in the commands on his console.

Starfall watched on as the *Marauder* shot a man-sized orb directly at the concussion missile.

Just before Starfall could see the impact, the ship cut a sharp turn behind the rear end of a nearby asteroid. The explosion lit the sides of the rock like the early beams of a sunrise.

"Our scanners show they are returning to Hesperia Ultima," Syntar said. "They think we've been destroyed."

"Good. Now get us to our destination."

Syntar nodded as his hands shifted on the controls.

The *Marauder* weaved through a labyrinth of asteroids, many long abandoned after years of drilling had left them stripped of resources. At least one asteroid, however, still had the signs of a lively mining operation: communications towers springing from the ground like oil derricks, and specks of light running along the landing platforms. Industrial lamps lit the small mining city in a bright blue wash. The long shadows of countless unmanned machines stretched out into nothingness.

As the *Marauder* flew past the northern edge of town, a deactivated drilling rig hung motionless above a two-kilometer-wide pit in the ground.

Starfall stared at the darkness below. It seemed to stretch forever. Something unsettling about it, she thought, as the ship sailed past the abyss.

Ahead, a cluster of steel bunkers near the southern edge of town made up the majority of the temporary mining colony.

"Here it is, Captain. Asteroid XB117," Syntar said.

"Good," she replied. "We're on time. Land the ship and keep your weapons close. The miners are a rough bunch. Some say isolation has led them to madness."

"We're no slouches in the crazy department either, Captain," said Caspian.

Starfall unsheathed a Bowie knife from her belt and traced the edge of the blade with her thumb and index finger. "I know," she said, smiling.

———∾———

The crew slipped into their pressure suits and attached their weapons within easy reach.

The ramp slid down with a hiss of compressed air. Syntar and Killborn lugged the sealed crates onto the hover-dolly and pushed it forward.

A small tremor rattled the ground beneath them.

"Be careful with the merchandise," said Starfall. "We don't want to spill any."

"I didn't figure this place was known for seismic activity," Killborn said.

"It's not," said Syntar. "There are no tectonic plates. This should be a dead rock."

The door to the nearest bunker opened. Two men in blue pressure suits, armed with power drills, stepped out. The drills made for dangerous close-range weapons and could puncture their suits with ease. Starfall touched the blaster at her side for reassurance.

The guards guided the crew past the airlocks. A loud hiss of compressed air tugged at their bodies.

Inside, a labyrinth of tight hallways and corridors comprised most of the bunker. As Starfall walked ahead with the two armed guards, she managed a few glances inside the miners' quarters. They consisted of cramped rooms with three bunkbeds stacked together in a claustrophobe's nightmare. Men with scarred faces and missing limbs stared back from the shadows. The hallway wound past more sleeping quarters, lavatories, and a dimly lit game room with a wall rack holding broken pool cues with red tips.

The lights flickered, and an electric buzz—like angered hornets— filled the air. Missing fixtures dotted the bunker, with meshes of exposed wires coiling out of the holes in the walls. Broken slats jutted out of the air-recycling vents along the ceiling.

The guards stopped outside a spacious mess hall and motioned the crew inside.

A tall, broad-shouldered man in olive fatigues and steel-toed boots stood in the center of the room, stroking his neatly cropped goatee. He tilted his head back as he observed the crew. A long white scar ran perpendicular along his neck.

"Captain Starfall," the man said in a low, raspy voice, "I am Overseer Falkner. I run the day-to-day operations here. I am so glad you made it past the blockade."

"We guarantee delivery," she said.

"So I've heard. The men are about to have dinner. I would be delighted if you joined us. We'll be having stew, biscuits, and grog. Perhaps you'll partake in some of the merchandise with us as well?"

"The merchandise?" asked Killborn.

"Yes," Falkner said, smiling. "If you wouldn't mind ingesting contraband psychedelics with my men, that is. They are psychoactive spores emitted from the *Locongo* flower found in the swamps of Hesperia Ultima. When inhaled, they produce a sense of euphoria. On occasion they can lead to strange visions, but I wouldn't worry about that."

"The *Locongo* spores are banned under Hesperia law," Caspian said. "It is a crime punishable by death."

"We have our own laws here. Besides, pirates like you have little regard for the law."

Killborn looked at the crates on the hover-dolly before turning to grin at Starfall.

Starfall smiled back. "Why not? We almost got killed on our way over here. A little stress relief couldn't hurt. Crew, unload the merchandise and get ready for dinner."

⁓

Starfall knocked back the mug; bitter, hoppy alcohol sloshed down her throat. She slammed the mug on the table, causing the empty plates around her to bounce.

Across the table, Killborn laughed at a miner's crude joke—his saliva mixing with grog as it trickled down his chin. Beside the deckhand, Caspian sipped his drink slowly, keeping one hand above his cutlass.

Rags Syntar played his electric sitar for the miners. The robot plucked the strings like a spider weaving a web.

All around her, Starfall heard the howls and cackles of revelry. Miners and pirates sat side by side on rotting wooden benches, ingesting the bitter piss-water they called grog. She couldn't help but scowl into her drink. Her darkened reflection scowled back.

"I'm glad you joined us," the gravelly voice behind her said. "Mind if I sit?"

Falkner managed a smirk.

"Of course," Starfall said.

"Nothing pleases me more than forging strong new relationships. You know, Starfall, certain materials are hard to come by here, with us being so far away from everything. We move from asteroid to asteroid, drilling for resources until we're ready to sell all we've reaped. Thankless work. Hesperia Ultima doesn't thank us. Neither do any of the other planets in the system. All we ask for is some decent food, some entertainment, and the occasional stress relieving... ingredients."

"Plenty of smugglers out there for that."

"We've tried others before."

"What happened to them?"

"Their corpses are probably floating aimlessly through space."

"Well, I'm glad we could help."

Falkner smiled again and motioned to his men. A small crew of miners retrieved one of the crates, gently rolling it beside Falkner.

"Shall we?" he asked, unclasping the lid. Falkner grabbed a handful of grey-green sand and threw it up, toward the vents. The pollen danced across the room, swaying in the currents of ventilated air.

The miners shoved their noses upward and inhaled, their chests expanding as the spores filled their lungs.

Killborn mimicked the miners and inhaled with an open mouth.

"What the hell?" Caspian said, placing a hand on the deckhand's shoulder. He closed his eyes and let the *Locongo* spores seep into his nose.

Falkner nodded at Starfall, a devious grin growing wider.

She took one last swig of grog. "Screw it, why not?" Starfall stood and sucked in a deep breath. The spores tickled her throat and nose as they shimmied their way down into her lungs. The fungus was odorless, and nearly undetectable.

Rags Syntar leaned against the wall as he played his sitar, the strings reverberating louder than before. The slow twang of steel slithered into her ears and brain, the universe vibrating to a relaxing rhythm.

The miners laughed—a collection of toothless maws and rotten gums, cackling like witches.

Time slowed. Every man in the room emanated a blurry aura. She felt at ease for the first time in a while. Boredom, loneliness—nothing seemed to exist at the moment. Only the sort of peace the dead must feel. Starfall smiled.

Just then she heard something. A subtle banging, like a baton on a faraway drum. Pounding. The sound was muffled like a distant heartbeat. *Boom. Boom. Boom.*

Was it her heart? No one else seemed to notice. Was it in her head? Then, an ominous sound, like distant ocean waves crashing against rocks. Voices in unison.

"Does anyone else hear that?"

Falkner smiled. This time it was genuine.

"You hear them?"

"I hear *something*," she said.

"Do you want to see them? It's our little secret down here."

She nodded.

"All of you are welcome to see," he said, motioning to her crew.

The tunnel entrance was near the end of the compound, by the equipment facilities. The miners had drilled through dense ashen-colored rock to make the tunnel. It plunged into the darkness of the ground itself. Ragged grooves spiraled through solid rock, leading to an unseen cavern. Falkner carried the lantern as he waited for Starfall's crew to enter.

"It's just down there," he said, flashing his teeth like a grinning dog. She wondered if it was a trap. Was he leading them down there to commit some heinous crime? She shook the thought from her head and continued onward.

The droning grew louder. A humming chorus occasionally broken up into staccato notes.

"I hear it now," Caspian said, wide-eyed.

"Me too," said Killborn, steadying himself against the tunnel walls. "It sounds like a hymn."

"I hear nothing," Syntar said, shuffling along behind them.

The farther she walked down the tunnel, the more it seemed the walls were closing in on her.

The crew followed her into the darkness, their steps echoing down the hole. The ground rumbled beneath their feet. Loose dirt sifted from the low ceiling of the tunnel, bathing them in dust and glittering minerals.

"Damn it to hell," Caspian said.

"Do not despair," Falkner said. "The walls will hold."

Farther down, the tunnel leveled out into a chamber with a path leading to a single wooden door. The voices stopped.

"What's in there?" Starfall asked.

"Take a peek," Falkner said, eyeing a sliding hatch on the door.

Starfall took a step forward. The sound of something shuffling along a dirty floor slithered under the door and into her ears. The *Locongo* flower had disrupted her senses. She felt like those times she'd sleepwalked as a little girl.

Starfall slid the hatch open and gasped.

A group of eight gangly humanoid creatures stood from crouched positions and scattered into the darkened corners of the cell. Their skin appeared a muddy-green hue, like that of the amphibians on numerous planets she'd explored. Their mouths reminded her of a piranha's, with tiny needle-like teeth jutting out from a terrible underbite.

Bulbous eyes stared back at her, glistening in the shadows.

She took a step back. Her men rushed to the hatch, shoving their faces against the small window, trying to catch a glimpse. Starfall knelt on the ground, a wave of nausea sweeping over her.

Falkner placed a hand on her shoulder. "'Banu Qasi,' they call themselves. They came from beyond the belt, beyond the star system. Refugees from some far off, war-torn place. We shot down their ship and imprisoned them here. We give them food and allow them to live as long as they behave and help us with mining operations."

"Behave?" said Starfall as she fell on one knee, fighting the urge to throw up.

"They are a treacherous lot," he said, running two fingers along the scar on his neck. He turned to Starfall just as she began to gag. "Oh. Captain, you don't look so good. Shall we get you to bed?"

Falkner's cackles echoed down the dark chambers. Then, the world went dark.

***

Starfall woke on a stiff cot. Her head pounded, and her spine spasmed with every breath she took. Snores filled the cramped, dark room. She peered over the edge of the bed. Below her, the rest of her crew slept like the dead, their limbs splayed out. Syntar had set himself on sleep mode beside a charging port on the wall. Starfall climbed down the bunk bed and stretched.

What had happened? Everything was a blur. The *Locongo* spores. That was it. Falkner said the spores gave one visions. She remembered the sight of green-skinned monsters, hunkered in the dark abyss of a cave, scuttling like vermin against the rocky walls, the nightmare sounds of an ominous hymn, the trembling of the earth beneath her feet. Everything felt like a hallucination.

But had it been? She peered outside the room. The hallway was dim and empty. There was only the faint sound of conditioned air blowing out the vents. Starfall stepped outside.

Maybe Falkner would have some answers. She hoped she hadn't embarrassed herself. She would apologize to him for anything her or her crew might have done while intoxicated.

The hallways were long and winding. Nothing, not even the sound of distant footfalls, echoed down the bunker. The mess hall had been meticulously cleaned; any evidence of the night's festivities had been wiped.

The temptation to turn back was strong. As was the yearning to revisit what she'd seen. Sierra Starfall had always been a curious woman. Since childhood, her inquisitiveness had tended to get her into trouble. No reason to stop now, she thought. She vaguely remembered the way to the tunnel. It was toward the back end of the bunker, near the storage rooms cluttered with busted rigs.

When she arrived, it was as she remembered. A long tunnel bored into the earth with what must have been a large drill. She stopped at the entrance of the tunnel, listening for the sounds she'd heard earlier in the night.

Nothing.

Starfall started down the tunnel, running her hands along the walls to keep from tripping in the dark.

She reached the bottom, finding the wooden door where it had been before. Her hands trembled as she slid the hatch open.

Nothing. Just the darkness of an empty cave. Starfall slid the locking bolt and threw the door open. She drew her blaster, keeping it readied at her side. The cave was cold, and the air was still.

The *Locongo* spores had made a fool of her. They had dulled her senses and clouded her judgment. The miners had probably laughed at Starfall and her crew. *Imbecile pirates, the lot of them.*

Starfall pivoted to turn away when she heard footsteps behind her. She swung around, bringing up the blaster. A group of green monsters stepped out from the shadows.

"Stay right there," she said.

One of the creatures took a step forward. Its green skin appeared discolored—wrinkled. It opened its mouth, exposing tiny, sharp teeth. It raised a webbed hand in the air.

We mean you no harm. The voice echoed in her mind.

"Who said that?"

The wrinkled creature tapped its chest. *I said that.*

"You can speak into my mind? No, this isn't happening. I must be coming down from the *Locongo* spores."

Your mind is on an open pathway to mine. You have not closed your mind as the others have. My name is Kiak, and I speak for my people, the Banu Qasi.

"No. Impossible. What are you?"

Alive.

"No, no—where do you come from?"

Our history is on the cave wall behind you.

She turned her head, keeping the blaster trained on Kiak. Behind her, white chalk marks were scrawled over the cave walls. Odd shapes and symbols she couldn't decipher. "I can't read that. Is that your language?"

Kiak nodded. *It is how I keep our history alive. I do it for the young ones,* he said, sweeping a hand over the rest of the group. *I have to erase it every night when the others arrive. They forbid our writing.*

"What? Why would they do that?"

Deny them their history, and you exterminate an entire culture's future.

"How did you end up here?"

We are refugees from the planet Qasan, far from this solar system. Our home was destroyed by a people known as the Zurabar. My family and I fled on a small ship. We were crossing this system's asteroid belt when the men of this colony shot us down. We are the only survivors. We are made to toil every day for our survival.

"Slaves."

Kiak nodded.

"I heard singing last night."

You heard our sacred hymns? Your mind must be very receptive. The leader of the men, he can hear us as well, but he closes himself off, resists us, uses torture to silence us.

We sing to the elder god we discovered living on this asteroid. It has become our deity, and it lives here, deep in the abyss. The elders are everywhere, even here.

"The elders?"

Gods born before the universe itself. They listen to us always, and protect us. Though not every elder is known to us, they are there, ever-present. And the elder of this asteroid hears our song every night as it slumbers.

Starfall felt something in her chest. She assumed it was pity. She wasn't sure; she'd rarely forged enough connections to remember what empathy felt like. "I don't know about any elders, but all I know is you can't live like this. I'm sure I can talk to Falkner and arrange something."

We have tried. My son attempted speaking with him. The man you call Falkner ended his existence.

"I saw a scar on his throat. Did your son cause that that?"

My son, in his death throes, reached a hand out, lacerating the man's flesh.

"I'm sorry for your loss, I-"

The earth quaked. The rumble nearly knocked Starfall off her feet. Rocks came loose from the cave ceiling.

"The tremors are getting worse," she said. "What's going on?"

That is the elder. We have been digging too deep into its home. The men refuse to listen. Any moment now the elder will wake from its slumber and break free from the shackles of the asteroid.

"Are you saying this rock is breaking apart?"

Kiak nodded. He took a step back toward the group. One of the Banu Qasi rubbed its stomach, its belly protruding like that of a pregnant human female.

"Are you... with child?" Starfall asked.

The Banu Qasi nodded. *I am Onessak. Life will blossom soon.*

"I can't leave you here. It's not right." Outside Starfall heard the faint scuffling of boots on the hallway floor. Perhaps one of the miners on guard. She holstered her blaster. "I'll be back for you soon. I promise." Starfall turned and locked the door behind her.

Through the slit in the hatch, she saw the elder Banu Qasi wipe the cave wall with his hand.

In the quiet of the tunnel, Sierra Starfall began to sob.

<p style="text-align:center">~~~</p>

She paced back and forth across the room.

"What are you saying, Captain?" Caspian asked. "Those monsters we saw last night were real?"

"Yes."

"I can confirm that," Syntar said. "I witnessed them as well. The spores do not affect me."

"The miners keep them as slaves?"

"That's right."

"Well, what's the big deal? It's not our problem." Killborn rubbed his temples, feeling the full weight of his hangover. "I say we leave 'em."

"Not an option," said Starfall.

"You don't mean we're going to try and save them? That'll get us killed!"

"That's exactly what we're going to do."

"Get killed?" Syntar asked.

"No, *save them*," said Starfall. "We just have to find a way. We're outnumbered here."

"Captain," Caspian said, "we've been through many adventures together. But I'm not sure we can pull this off."

Starfall crossed her arms across her chest. "We have the luxury of freedom. The luxury of doing whatever the hell we want. Those people down there don't. We're no saints, but we're also not blind. I can't ignore what I saw down there."

The crew fell silent. The sounds of miners rousing and marching toward the showers filled the hallways.

"Well, we've committed our share of wrongs before," Caspian said. "Maybe if we do this the scales of karma will tip back in our favor. What do you say, crew?"

Overseer Falkner walked through the doorway. He tapped a blaster at his side. "Good morning, everyone. I hope you all slept well. I couldn't help but overhear-"

Syntar swung his sitar across Falkner's face, the instrument shattering into pieces of wood and steel coil. Falkner collapsed at the doorway.

"I'll get the ship ready," Syntar said. "You just figure out what you have to do, Captain."

"Right. Thanks."

The robot marched ahead.

"Killborn," Starfall barked, "drag his body in here and tie him down. Caspian, I'm going to need your help. I've got an idea."

∼∼∼

Starfall struggled to balance on Caspian's back as Killborn handed her the crate. She lifted the container and tipped it carefully into the vent.

"We may inadvertently inhale some of the stuff, but oh well," she said.

She poured the entirety of the *Locongo* spores into the vent, the fan sucking up most of the pollen-sized fungus.

"In a few minutes, this structure will be full of armed miners on psychedelics. Stay alert. I'm gonna release the Banu Qasi from their cell." Starfall hopped off Caspian's back and ran toward the tunnel.

"Aye," Caspian said, drawing his cutlass from its scabbard, "we've got your back, Captain."

Starfall ran down the tunnel, her hands guiding her in the dark. The ground trembled and moaned below her boots. She steadied herself against the cave walls until the shaking stopped. When she reached the bottom, she kicked the door open. The wood splintered into a dozen pieces. The Banu Qasi clutched each other's arms as they pressed their backs against the rocky walls of their cell.

"All of you, come with me," Starfall said. "I'm getting you out of here."

Eight Banu Qasi followed her up the dark path. The sound of blaster fire echoed in the distance. At the mouth of the tunnel, Caspian and Killborn fired their blasters at a group of miners across the hall. At their feet lay three men with crimson slashes decorating their backs.

"Come on, Captain," Caspian shouted, "we have to leave."

"Lead the way," she said.

Caspian and Killborn charged ahead, shooting madly at the throng of gathering miners. The smell of ozone and singed flesh was overwhelming. Starfall covered her nose with one hand. As she turned, she saw the Banu Qasi clearly for the first time under the halogen lights. They had no noses. Their skin was moist and semi-transparent. Open bruises oozed across their flesh like a pox. She felt a wave of pity sweep over her again. But, more than anything, she felt purpose.

An alarm rang out across the compound, blaring through hidden speakers. White lights switched to a deep red. The sound pierced her ears and drilled through her head. Beads of sweat dripped down her forehead. Starfall couldn't tell if the ground was quaking again, but her feet trembled all the same. The spores were disrupting her motor functions.

The crew sprang down the maze of hallways, running past the dining hall and the run-down rec room.

A lone miner thrust out from one of the sleeping quarters as Starfall marched past. He tackled her to the floor and wrested the blaster from her grip. Starfall slid a hand down her thigh and unclasped the Bowie knife from its sheath. The man pointed the blaster at Kiak. Starfall raised her knees and bucked the man forward, disrupting his aim. She plunged the knife into his side. He spasmed on the floor like a fish before dying.

Above, Kiak offered an outstretched hand. Starfall accepted it and nodded. He heaved her up and placed a hand on his chest before bowing slightly.

"Are you alright, Captain?" asked Caspian.

"Come on," she said, ignoring the question, "we're close to the entrance."

The vents hissed and spat out a fine ashen dust. A few miners sat with their faces buried in their knees, rocking back and forth as they succumbed to the psychedelics.

Ahead, the entrance door was sealed.

"Damn," Killborn said. "We don't have a way of opening it."

"No pressure suits, either," said Caspian.

The loud, furious shriek of machinery buzzed behind their backs. Falkner stood in a pressure suit, cradling a power drill like a rifle in his arms. The large drill bit spun in a dizzying blur. Falkner eyed the group of pirates and slaves with rage. His visor had fogged, obscuring most everything but his eyes.

"You monsters aren't leaving alive," Falkner said, raising his drill. "I should've known you spacers were planning some treachery."

Caspian and Killborn raised their blasters. Falkner slapped his wrist. The doors slid open. Depressurized air tugged at Starfall's clothing with a hiss. The cold vacuum of the asteroid's atmosphere yanked the crew and the Banu Qasi off their feet and sucked them outside like rag dolls. Starfall clung to a set of guard rails on the wall. Falkner slapped his wrist again and the doors sealed shut.

Starfall dropped to the floor. The world spun. Slowed down.

"I want you to do me a favor, Captain," Falkner said, stepping forward. "In your last breaths I want you to describe what this feels like." The drill spun again, buzzing like a colony of bees. Starfall crouched low to the ground, her legs coiled like springs. In the corner of her eye, she spotted it, glistening like the jewels that used to catch her fancy. Caspian's cutlass.

Falkner's stride turned into a full sprint. He raised the power drill and jousted toward her midsection. Starfall snatched the cutlass and took a step back toward the entrance door. She drew her arm back, cocking the cutlass for a downward slash. If the drill caught any part of her flesh, she'd be torn to shreds. She would have to duck at the last second and swiftly counter to one of Falkner's limbs.

Her head pounded. The spores were in full effect. Falkner's body warped into a distorted combination of colors and shapes. *Focus.* The sound of the drill. It grew closer. A few feet away now. She readied the blade. Falkner lunged forward. Her legs bent slightly. Now or never.

Just then, the ground quaked. The floorboards cracked apart and the ceiling tore open, cables spilling out like disemboweled guts. Falkner lost balance and momentum carried him forward. The drill sailed past Starfall's head and lodged itself in the door. As Falkner tried to pull the drill out, Starfall brought the cutlass down on his forearm.

His right arm dropped to the floor.

Overseer Falkner let loose a howl muffled by his mask. Starfall kicked in the back of his kneecap, and the overseer dropped to the ground. She drew the blade back and brought it down on his neck. The screaming stopped.

Starfall dropped the blade and inhaled a deep breath. She shut her eyes, hoping to stop the shaking in her mind. When she opened her eyes again, the floor lay in ruins. Asteroid XB117 was on the verge of collapse.

She looked around. The crew! She reached for Falkner's severed arm and pressed the button on his wrist. The airlock doors slid open, tearing apart the drilling tool. The vacuum pulled violently at her body. She let herself be yanked away. She landed outside, skidding on the rugged ground.

She gasped for breath as the chill air stung her skin like a million needles. Her crew was nowhere to be seen. She closed her eyes and waited for the darkness to take her. She'd laughed in Death's face before. Now it was time for Death to collect on her bounty.

Above, the loud whir of thrusters burning through the air. The *Marauder* swung low, ramp extended. Caspian and Killborn were at the tail end of the ramp, hands outstretched. She stood and took both hands. They hoisted her up and walked her up the ramp before it sealed shut behind them. She gasped and hacked as she cleared her throat and clean oxygen once again flowed through her lungs.

The Banu Qasi approached Starfall and formed a circle around her. They bowed their heads and embraced her gently. Like family.

Below, deep fissures splintered across the asteroid, splitting the terrain apart.

"Syntar, get us out," yelled Starfall as she turned to her helmsman. The robot nodded.

The *Marauder* shot vertically into the air, thrusters at full power. The Banu Qasi lost balance, spilling over like bowling pins.

A massive sinkhole opened beneath the colony. The facility's communication towers tumbled into the dark depths below. Like tiny flecks of black, the miners were swallowed by the dark maw like ants in a flood.

"Look, Captain," Caspian said, pointing out the bow window. All around the *Marauder*, hundreds of asteroids began to crack apart. Wide fissures zigzagged across their rocky exteriors. Their surfaces exploded, shooting plumes of sediment into space.

Nestled inside the core of every exposed asteroid sat what appeared to be large transparent spheres filled with a gelatinous substance. Starfall rubbed her eyes. The spores were still manipulating her mind. Had to be.

Two black ovals pressed against the inside of each membrane. Some even seemed to be tracking the *Marauder*'s flight. The giant sacs burst simultaneously, the liquid shooting off into space in every direction.

Hundreds of anomalies stared at the *Marauder* as the ship hovered in space. Their bodies resembled those of baby chicks: long, pointed beaks; bulbous black eyes; naked wings wrapping around their bellies. They looked... premature. Like things neglected by nature and left to die.

They have woken, Kiak said. He stared in awe, a hand reaching for the air in front of him. The Banu Qasi kneeled and bowed their heads. The crew watched in silence.

"Are you seeing what I'm seeing?" asked Killborn after some time.

Caspian stood alongside him, placing a gentle hand on Killborn's shoulder. "Aye, lad. Aye."

Some of the birds began to move their heads and uncoil their wings. Others lay motionless, floating in a lifeless drift as starlight lit their stillborn bodies.

"Some of them are dead," said Starfall.

"A result of the mining operations," Syntar said.

"Yeah. Something tells me we woke them early."

The Banu Qasi began to chant, an audible hum this time. An ancient prayer to ancient beings.

"Give us some room, Syntar," said Starfall. "Move us slowly away from here." Syntar nodded. The *Marauder* jetted away.

The birds that were still alive craned their necks, their heads gazing curiously at the passing ship. One by one, they extended their limbs and drifted slowly apart in every direction. Birds the size of asteroids. Starfall couldn't believe it. Could anyone?

"Imagine how beautiful they would have been," she said, looking upon the stillborn elders drifting in the void. Starfall looked upon the Banu Qasi as they held hands in prayer. Life went on. Starfall turned toward the chicks spreading their wings. "And yet... imagine how beautiful they will be, still."

Dracosaurus Reborn

Dr. Charles Levy and assistant Winston Schulz hunched over the computer screen in the pitch hours of the night.

"The specimen appears ready. Open the tube, Winston."

"Yes, Doctor."

The tube hissed; compressed oxygen erupted outward.

Both doctors endeavored for years obtaining the perfect, preserved DNA sample of the newly discovered Dracosaurus.

Its body shifted.

Having the body of a T-Rex, and most shockingly: large wings.

Its eyes opened.

To breathe new life into Dracosaurus would be to open new possibilities.

Its wings stretched.

The scientific marvel of it!

It towered over the doctors.

"Dude...we cloned a dragon."

Then fire.

Legacy

Alejandro Brazo knew he was as good as dead. Though, he wasn't sure that it mattered anymore. It was over and he knew it and *they* knew it and if there was a God, he knew it, too.

They'd spotted him. Before they could fire off a shot, he had managed to dash past the library's main entrance and quickly fasten the doors behind him. The doors were large and heavy, but what was wood to their laser cannons?

Alejandro leaned against a bookshelf, his lungs burning as he huffed. He wiped his glasses with the tail of his shirt. Everything was blurry and nothing made sense. The world was the same way. It all happened so quickly it could be argued that nothing had happened at all. And if it did there would be no one to record it. Everyone was gone. Wiped out like vermin in the dead of night.

Invaders from outer space. Alejandro's hand trembled as he slid his glasses over the bridge of his nose. He remembered the news broadcasts vividly before the world went dark. They were called Taurans, conquerors from beyond our solar system. From the cold void between the stars. Before long, Earth's armed forces were subjected to a slaughter. And when the monsters made landfall, they ripped every child from their mothers' arms and burned down every book in every library, collectively destroying Earth's past and future. Fitting that he locked himself in a library now.

His hand pulsed to the beat of his heart. A gash ran the length of his palm all the way down his wrist. He supposed he was lucky to be alive. Or was it cursed? He'd hidden beneath the wreckage of crushed cars amidst the rubble of Mexico City. Sometimes he'd even play dead as patrolling Taurans swept the vicinity. In the weeks after the attack, though, Alejandro hadn't spotted a single survivor.

But this time they'd seen him. He was feeble and old and couldn't run as fast as he used to.

And here he was. The National Library of Mexico. Over 7,500 square meters spread over three sprawling floors: a wealth of human records cataloguing mankind's triumphs, failures, sins, and farces. It was a vault of information, of myth and fact. The archives chronicling where Man had traversed; a snapshot of the clay that molded him.

Now all that information would burn and scatter with the wind. Nothing to leave behind. He felt a weight on his shoulders. A responsibility to his ancestors to keep the flame alive, no matter how rough the winds blew.

Alejandro stood upright. His back ached and his legs felt like concrete. The effects of time making its presence known to him. *Stupid old man.*

As he shuffled through the main hall, he ran his hand across the rows of towering bookshelves. The smooth oak shelves had accumulated layers of dust. The library had fallen into disarray with no one left to maintain it. No one left to read the books or stamp the cards. No one left to hush discourteous conversations or to answer queries. He had inherited sole stewardship now.

Alejandro waded into the Classic Literature section and ran his index finger across the spines of old books; a world of textures brushed against his skin. Some were leathery and rough, others were smooth and flat. He picked out a book at random. *Don Quixote* by Miguel de Cervantes. A classic. One he loathed as a child. It was an intimidatingly large book for an eight-year-old boy. But as a college student, he'd reacquainted himself with it like a former lover. A grand epic of adventure and satire. The story: a man bored with life, inspired by the novels he cherished, taking up arms and creating adventures in his mind, all to fill his life with some sense of meaning. He opened the book and perused the card on the front flap. It hadn't been stamped in seven years. He felt a pull inside his chest. Why had it been so long since its last checkout? Had people given up on the most endearing works of fiction? He remembered reading in the newspaper that youth had traded books for phones; fiction for gossip; news for tabloids; authors for celebrities; wisdom for chatter. If that was the case, society had condemned itself to death long before the celestial invaders.

He placed the book back and sighed. He ascended to the third floor, strolling past computers and large lacquered tables. He switched on all the desk lamps in the hopes he wouldn't feel so alone. To his surprise the power still worked. Perhaps some generators had kicked in. He told himself he wasn't the last man in Mexico City; he was just the last student, studying long into the night before an exam; long after everyone else had left for the warmth of their beds. Just like college.

He peered over the ledge. His wrinkled hands gripped the railing as he looked upon the large entrance door. He wasn't afraid of dying. He was old and he knew that his days were up. What scared him was that he now held the distinct honor of being the world's oldest person, while also being its youngest. He was the last of the lineage of thinkers and butchers. Yes, human beings were the ultimate hypocrites, indeed.

There came the sound of distant rattling. Loose sediment rained on his head.

Any moment now. He played it in his head. They would blast through the doors, dash up the stairs, and trample his old bones to dust. He had no chance against their colossal frames, their silver blades, their cannons of light and fire. He felt guilty. He had been raised in a culture that believed strongly in resistance. The Mexican was born from the ashes of conquest, and thusly sowed the seeds of his own revolution and, ultimately, his freedom. Hell, that was written in every human history. Revolt. Change. Progress.

Alejandro wanted to fight back. To make a stand and claim his final moments as his own. Outnumbered or not, he knew he had to do something.

He turned around. Like rows of large dominos, the bookshelves stood guard. They resembled proud warriors, keeping the books safe and organized.

Alejandro never had children. He cycled through lovers and heartbreak over the years, but his seed never sprouted. His legacy was dead and wilted, never to be remembered. Was this what it came to? Just a flash-in-a-pan life, doomed to be forgotten by a warmongering species?

He refused to believe that. The imagination and tenacity of the human spirit was greater than the flesh and bones of an old man. He felt a spark in his head. *Don Quixote.* He smiled.

Tonight, he would make a statement. He would make the Taurans remember. He was going to challenge the giants with an arsenal of mankind's greatest ideas.

He shuffled towards the tables. First, he was going to need a weapon.

Alejandro picked up a chair and flipped it upside down. He kicked in one of its legs until it snapped off. He pulled a small knife from his pocket and rolled up his sleeves. He sat on the floor and ran the blade through the end of the wooden leg until it started taking shape. When he finished, he'd crafted a weapon that had slayed the most ancient of monsters. It felt good in his hands; possibly as good as they had felt in Abraham Van Helsing's hands. He sheathed the wooden stake in his belt and marched toward the office.

He came to the door and nudged it open. The copy machine stared back at him. He opened the machine and retrieved a ream of paper from its maw. He was going to need an air force and an army. He sat at one of the large, lacquered tables and set to work. He tried his best to steady his shaky hands; they were not the mason's hands they used to be. He was delicate and patient, folding the paper on itself, overlapping it multiple times, making sure every crease was perfect, every line properly straightened.

When he'd finished, he had a standing army of fifty origami men: perfect little replicants, all of them. He wondered if Phillip K. Dick would be proud. He wondered if the origami men dreamed, as he had.

He set the replicants aside and pinched and folded the remaining sheets of paper. He creased them as he did when he was a child. It was the first toy he ever had: the paper airplane. It was the airplane that started the gears of his imagination turning. His mind traveled back in time. He'd found his first hero when he'd read *The Fun of It*, Amelia Earhart's captivating memoir accounting her wonderful travels. And now he had a squadron of his own.

He placed his paper creations into a book bag and made his way back downstairs, placing the little men in ranks and files on the floor ten paces from the entrance. He had reinforcements, but he needed to slow the Taurans down; he needed a defensive wall. Alejandro tried to think. What had he read about setting up defenses? Then it came to him. Literature's greatest wall. *The Iliad* was mandatory reading in high school.

Alejandro planted his legs, placed his hands on the nearest bookshelf, and pushed. Books toppled as the shelf slid against the door.

His bones ached and his heart beat like a war drum. But it was worth it. His Trojan wall.

He sat by his soldiers and caught his breath. He was tired and wanted desperately to close his eyes.

The door pounded. Outside, muffled murmurs and shouts. The door pounded again, and the wood cracked like thunder.

They would eradicate him and set fire to the books, eliminating human history once and for all. It was the ultimate desecration. A fate worse than death from which there was no afterlife. Already all the world's digital files had surely been wiped. This was it. He was now the last man; he was Robert Neville. He was the protector of books; he was Guy Montag. He was the lone oppressed agitator; he was Winston Smith. Tonight would be his legacy; tonight, they would know the unbreakable human spirit; tonight, they would know Alejandro Brazo.

He ran up the third floor, trying to quell the fire in his lungs. *Breathe.* Tiny black spots began to fill his vision. He shook his head and carried forth.

The books became a blur as he darted past, but he made out a few titles: *The Jungle Book*; *The Art of War*; *Animal Farm*; *Frankenstein*; *Lolita*; *Dune*; *The Diary of Anne Frank*. All of them were his companions and they were cheering him on. They cheered for their champion as a newfound energy coursed through his veins.

When he arrived, he peered over the ledge. The best seat in the house.

An explosion. Wood splintered across the hall. Armored conquerors marched past the screen of smoke. Suddenly, they stopped. The wall lurched above them, casting a shadow over their bodies. They shot at the shelf, and paper and leather flew skyward. But the oak held. Alejandro reached into his book bag and pulled out a paper plane. He tossed it high and watched it spiral slowly downward. It struck one of the lieutenants in the shoulder. The others made a series of squeals that Alejandro understood to be laughter. The embarrassed lieutenant looked upon Alejandro and growled. The soldiers pushed the shelves in unison. Alejandro reached into his bag and slung the planes as fast as his hands would let him. The paper contraptions bounced off armor harmlessly, but the grunts and growls let him know that weak egos were something metal could never guard against.

They toppled the shelf over and the crash rattled the library. They scampered over the splintered wood like a blizzard of angry fire ants. The paper replicants awaited them on the ground. The Taurans came to a dead stop. They seemed to discuss something amongst themselves, as if the replicants themselves might be landmines or booby traps. They raised their blasters and obliterated the paper men. Their ashes flew in the air like snowfall. The world's last party.

The Tauran soldiers charged up the staircase. A few of the grunts began the process of burning the books and shooting the computers. Like the burning of the Library of Alexandria. Brave new world, indeed.

He awaited them. Everything had led to this point. The final encounter. What would the legacy of the human race amount to in its last gasps? What last words would be spoken? And would it matter with no one to record it? Would Alejandro's memory live on? Mankind stood for many things, but all that mattered was that knowledge was passed down, that we learn from our mistakes.

The lieutenant unsheathed a curved blade and approached the old man in glasses.

"You will remember me. You will remember all of us. Immortality takes many forms."

The Tauran stepped forward and raised the blade, shaking off the words like paper airplanes.

The old man unsheathed the wooden stake and yelled, "Viva la revolución!" and brought the point down on the Tauran's exposed neck. The creature yelped and dropped to the ground. The soldiers stared and growled in confusion. One of the Tauran soldiers stepped forward and curled its lips. It flashed its teeth, raised its rifle, and shot a bolt of energy through Alejandro's heart.

In moments, the body of Alejandro Brazo burned alongside the books. Their ashes intermingled so that they were one, and together they scattered and blew in the air.

The civil war escalated in flames. The Tauran Colonialists had surrounded the ambassador's compound on Earth. A line of Tauran Loyalists walked out in single formation with arms raised. Commander Taloset led his unit inside the compound. It was as much a military post as it was a decadent palace. It filled him with rage. The people had to learn about this. This could not stand. The Loyalists had been making slaves of the Tauran Colonialists on Earth for generations while they lived in luxury.

Ambassador Vrago sauntered towards Taloset in flowing red robes. The silver-tongued politician had erected the Slave Law, having drawn up the legislation himself. Ignorance had kept the Colonialists crippled. The uneducated workers droned through life, never knowing any better. But that would change. Taloset would ensure that the proper literature be dispensed across the planet. Information would be free to all.

"Taloset, my friend. I am glad you have come to make a deal. You will be a very wealthy Tauran by the end of all of this. A very important Tauran. Then, when the time comes, we can throw your Colonialist friends by the wayside."

Taloset looked up in seething rage. He raised his blade like an offering to his ancestors. He thought about the enigmatic words his father had yelled whenever he was about to strike him or his siblings, the obscenity synonymous with angry retaliation. He brought the weapon down and yelled, "Viva la revolución!" The weighted blade crunched down on the ambassador's skull.

Taloset turned away from the dead ambassador and marched outside. He faced the cheering rebels. A new world awaited. One of transparency and transcendence. A world where knowledge, not weapons nor slavery, meant power.

The sun began to set across the horizon, and the ashes fell across the sky like snowfall.

The Facsimile War

First there was darkness. He was only vaguely aware of it, but it felt as if he'd been floating on the gentle tides of an unending ocean of black. Like a whisper, there came the faint sound of a distant explosion. He didn't know how long, but sometime later, a shockwave washed over him, rattling him into being. His heart began to hammer against his ribs, and he knew then he'd been alive.

He opened his eyes and gasped. Cool, filtered oxygen filled his lungs, extinguishing the fire in his chest. Once his breathing stabilized, his heart settled back into rhythm.

All around, a string of bright lights winked at him. Everything was blurry, distorted, like viewing the world through a window on a rainy day.

He rubbed his eyes, clearing away a thin film of moisture. The halo of blinding lights dimmed and the world began to come into focus. He raised a hand in front of his face and counted five long digits. One by one he curled them shut and open again, allowing himself to explore the limits of his motor functions. A shiver ran along his spine and the hairs on his body turned prickly. He was aware now that he stood naked inside a cylinder of chrome and glass.

He looked about his surroundings. He'd been on the tail end of a long file of about two dozen pods just like his, all of them lined against a wall. Each pod contained a single nude man or woman. One by one, they all stirred like children waking from a nap with mouths all agape. Beyond the glass lay a spacious, sterile room lined with rows of cots and bleeping, blinking terminals.

A med bay.

There came a gleam and a blur of movement off the glass. His eyes locked on his own reflection. Tired brown eyes stared back inquisitively. He was a man of average height sporting shortly cropped hair. His body was a tapestry of tattoos and scars upon dark skin. The markings on his limbs and torso consisted mostly of illegible cursive scrawl and the portraits of women, all unfamiliar to him. Family? Lovers?

He shook his head. Where was he? Who was he? He pressed his eyelids shut and tried to think. Nothing. No memories. Only an empty void.

Footsteps echoed outside the cylinder. A tall blond man in olive military fatigues approached his pod and tapped the glass with the corner of a PDA.

"Felix, can you hear me?" the man said in a muffled voice.

His mouth opened but no words came. He tried again. His lips were dry, and he tasted wet copper on his tongue. He pushed out a gurgle from the depths of his throat.

The man in fatigues nodded. "Your name is Felix Amaya. Thirty-two years old. Earth-born. De-atomized six years ago and rematerialized today on planet Ruun. You are a volunteer in the Terran Coalition Army under two-year contract. That is all the personal information that will be provided to you during your time here."

Another explosion shook the world. This time the sound was clearer, closer. After a brief moment, a shockwave rattled his cylinder. The lights on the rafters above swayed forcefully.

The man in fatigues grimaced. "Prepare for briefing and welcome to the war, Private Amaya."

The glass walls of the cylinder hissed and spun like a revolving door, opening the world up to him.

He placed a timid foot forward and felt the bite of cold air on his skin. Outside, the world thundered, and Felix Amaya knew fear.

⁘

After he'd received a series of inoculations, Felix found himself in line, shivering with the rest of the newly woken recruits. They were lined outside the med bay like cattle, a number of armed guards walking in stride, their batons at the ready. Lab technicians looked on as the naked parade marched down the sterile halls and into the adjacent washroom.

The warm waters of the shower woke him from his stupor, returning to him a clearer sense of awareness. His heart ached, then, as if struck by some sense of longing. There was something wrong, something missing, though what it was he couldn't quite decipher. He shook the thought and exited the showers. Once they were clothed, the recruits were brought to a small screening room where a pre-recorded holovid played for them. It was a video produced for newbies like him; *Blank Slates*, the officers had called them.

The holographic image of an old, frail man materialized in the center of the room. He introduced himself as the Administrator and bowed. The old man recounted a brief history of the colony in which the recruits now stood. Ages ago, the man said, six generation ships departed Earth, dispersing across the galaxy on a mission to discover and colonize new worlds. The inhabitants of the generation ship Alpha discovered planet Ruun, a world with a diverse topography and an equally rich biodiversity.

The first colonists named the settlement Sarkov's Landing, in honor of a Captain Gustavo Sarkov, whose shuttle was the first to touch down safely after previous failed attempts. From there the settlement budded outward into a municipal complex of schools, hospitals, barracks, dwellings, and farms, all spanning ten kilometers up and across.

The colony was nestled on the northwestern portion of a rich valley at the base of the jagged Akkavian mountain range which ran along the northern borders of its location. The rich valley was thickly canvased by tall grass three meters high, along with an abundance of distinct flora and fauna making the area suitable for human habitation.

Felix wanted to shut his eyes and doze off. But the man droned on. After Alpha emptied its cargo of supplies and half-a-million people, all that remained was a skeleton crew left to man what had become a massive surveillance and communication satellite as it orbited the planet.

And with that the Administrator finally fizzled out of existence.

Felix wondered what this all had to do with him, wanting desperately to ask the old man a few questions. He tried again to remember even the slightest of details. He couldn't. Not the name of his mother, or if he'd owned a dog, nothing that indicated who he was other than the color of his skin and the pigment etched on his body.

They were led through the barracks and inside a cluster of cutting-edge air hangars. They were spacious and industrial, and Felix would have liked to admire them if they hadn't been buzzing with urgency. Everywhere he turned, soldiers marched hastily, their rifles clutched to their chests. The pinwheel sparks of welding torches lit the catwalks and rafters above as mechanics toiled away on a slew of military crafts. Medics carted in scores of wounded troops whose faces resembled ground meat. Worse still had been the sirens as they blared across the hallways, their piercing screeches making his head throb.

He couldn't remember if he'd ever been in the military. Everything seemed strange yet familiar. His subconscious gnawed at him, memories surely, trying to scratch their way to the surface.

They were shepherded into a mess hall. Sullen-eyed workers slid them plastic trays, their meals consisting of milk, bread rolls, canned meat, and what appeared to be enigmatic root vegetables mashed into a purple puree.

Felix pushed his tray aside. He wasn't hungry. A wave of nausea had come over him and he wondered if it had to do with the vaccine they'd administered. The skin on his right shoulder began to bruise and swell at the sight of the inoculations. The doctors told him it would take a few days for the stuff to kick in. Something about rabies or infected saliva that caused hallucinations and disease. He rubbed his shoulder and winced. Soreness had started to creep in.

A red-haired woman sat across the table from him. The tattoo of a grinning infant adorned her left arm. The name *Curtis* had been spelled in block letters just below the child's portrait. The baby was a chubby-cheeked cherub that had the woman's eyes; large, wondrous, and full of life. She prodded her food with a fork. He offered her a smile. She smiled back. Her face suddenly contorted as if she wanted to ask him something, something personal or painful, perhaps. Before she could ask, she turned away.

The other recruits sat in silence, most of them ogling their food inquisitively.

When mealtime was over, a pair of armed guards marched them into an empty assembly hall. The guards ordered the recruits to stand at attention, which had surprisingly come naturally to him.

The assembly hall had been adorned with the flags of the Terran Coalition; the image of planet Earth orbited by six smaller spheres forming a ring amidst a backdrop of black. Toward the front of the hall, a podium sat dusty and dilapidated, clearly unused in years.

A large screen near the podium powered on.

The scrambled transmission of a silver-haired man clad in full combat armor came alive. To his back, a crimson moon hung over an orange sky. Great plumes of smoke blanketed the mountains stretching along the northern horizon. The man quickly assessed his new recruits before speaking. "I am Field Commander Wesley Nolan," the man said, snarling. A long scar ran up his chin, through his lips, and ended just above his left eye, which was now just a milky, lifeless orb. His face appeared fractured and hastily reconstructed, like a poorly assembled jigsaw puzzle. "Everything I say, I say once, so pay close attention, because we face extinction and time is not a luxury we can afford."

Extinction? Felix felt his heart drop into his stomach.

Outside, the explosions continued, their distant vibrations travelling up his spine.

"As you've already been briefed," Nolan said, "six generation ships departed Earth, scattering out across the galaxy on a mission to explore and colonize new planets."

Nolan leaned into a shoulder radio, barking unintelligible commands.

"Centuries later," Nolan continued, "when those ships arrived at their destinations, they established teleportation relays to thread the needle between our worlds."

A flash of red light lit the sky. The feed cut out momentarily before returning to normal.

"Through these relays, physical objects could be atomically deconstructed and rearranged into pure data. The data would then be beamed across space, received, and reproduced via specialized quantum printers. Tools, food, people. Materials colonists needed desperately for survival. For the war. That is how you all arrived here. But I'm going to be blunt," Nolan said, his face softening. "Every single one of you has died on your journey here."

A few of the younger recruits gasped. Felix felt his insides churn, but he made no effort to show his displeasure.

Nolan rested his rifle on his shoulder. "You are only carbon copies. Facsimiles. The de-atomization of organic matter destroys the subject completely. When its genetic data becomes reassembled, neither consciousness nor memories can be restored. Bio-chemical codes are a complex component of the brain and the science behind organic teleportation has yet to be mastered. Only certain motor functions that have been hardwired into the brain may be retained. Memory consolidation, they call it. Muscle memory, to be exact. Which is why you've all been thoroughly trained prior to your arrival. You do not remember any of this, but those instincts are deeply ingrained into your being and will serve you well out here."

Felix glanced at his palms. They had turned sweaty. He flipped them over. The back of his right hand was marked by a cross. The faded green tattoo showed the wear of time as it nearly melded into the dark brown of his skin.

Dead? A carbon copy? He wanted to shout, curse at Nolan, anything other than stand there like a fool.

He felt warm tears pooling along his eyelids. What was happening? His face flustered as the nausea returned. He inhaled a deep breath and allowed himself to regain his composure.

Nolan repositioned the camera and swept a hand over the fires raging behind him. A barrage of glimmering rockets streaked across the sky, carpeting the earth in the distance. A few seconds later the shockwaves shook the barracks. "We stand on planet Ruun," Nolan continued, "where we find ourselves entangled in an exhaustive, drawn-out battle with its natives: a race of bloodthirsty beings who perpetuate a war culture unlike any we've ever known. For nearly a hundred years now, we've fought them at our colony's doorstep. But our grasp is fading, and manpower has dwindled. That is why you are here."

A transport ship dropped in swiftly behind Nolan, its jet streams blasting the earth, blanketing the air in dust. It lowered itself into a controlled hover until it settled gently on the ground. A side panel slid upward. Inside, rows of armed soldiers sat fastened to thick harnesses as they awaited their commander.

"You were all former convicts on Earth. Each of you has agreed to a plea deal which will spare your life in return for your resolute service to a cause grander than yourselves. As of today, you are reborn. It does not matter what you did in your past life. What matters is what you do for your race, today. You now serve the Terran Coalition Army. Upon completion of your contract, you will be rewarded your freedom and a chance to rejoin society as colonists on Ruun."

Field Commander Nolan vaulted inside the carrier and faced the new recruits one last time. "You're all hitting the floor running, troops. Tonight's your first combat mission. Good luck out there."

The ship darted toward the fiery night and the transmission died.

Felix, along with most of the Blank Slates, retched on the floor.

⁓

"Move it, killers," the officer shouted, circling his finger in the air. "The vamps are running night assault!"

"Vamps?" Felix found himself asking aloud.

"You'll be briefed at the deployment bay," the officer said. "Keep it moving, killer."

They wasted little time corralling the new recruits into the armory. Blank Slates mingled with veterans, whose own distinct tattoos—teardrops, shamrocks, Scandinavian runes, gang names— marked them as former prisoners. Facsimiles.

Felix was quickly fitted with black form-hugging thermals embedded with electrodes and so much circuitry running through them, they resembled a vascular system.

Next, a cumbersome combat jacket was fastened over his torso. Some synthetic alloy-filament hybrid meant to protect against projectiles and bladed weapons just the same.

They fixed him with a *smart helmet*. Once the helmet was secured on his head, Felix instinctively flicked a small switch on the side. A visor slid over the brim and a HUD display flickered to life. Through his eyes he toggled through various sight modes: infrared, aim assist, airstrike targeting.

Lastly, the armorers dispensed the hyper-ballistic rifles, which propelled armor-piercing rounds at six times the speed of sound on account of the weapon's electromagnetic propulsion system. The techno-jargon had eluded Felix, and for some reason he'd suspected things like that always had.

Once the recruits had suited up, they were marched toward the barracks' eastern wing, where the deployment bay housed transport ships, bombers, surveillance drones, and armored track vehicles.

Scores of troops sprinted in and out of the eastern wall, where the fumes were so thick, all Felix could see was red smoke. He crinkled his nose. Hints of sulfur, methane, and other foul gasses permeated the air.

The Blank Slates were arranged behind a broken yellow line that stretched across the entire bay. A new CO approached them, scrutinizing them in silence. Then, one by one they were intermingled with veterans and assigned their duties.

Felix heard terms like *fire team, scout, demolitions.* None of them sounded particularly enticing.

The CO looked Felix over. "This one's scrawny. Get him on a turret, and far away from my ground forces."

Felix was promptly paired with the redhead from the mess hall and rolled over into a gunship crew.

They scrambled toward the staging area where a pair of gunships powered on, their jets whirring and spewing a vortex of hot air beneath their bellies. His assigned gunship was small, black, sleek, and resembled a cross between a rotorless Apache helicopter and a stealth bomber. There was a machine gun turret attached to either side of the ship's bay doors. The tip of the craft housed a front-mounted rocket launcher. Twin UV spotlights sat atop the roof just behind the cockpit.

He clambered over the side of the ship. The redhead smiled at him and leapt aboard next. A single pilot manned the ship, his hands manically flipping switches on the control panel as he whistled an ancient Motown tune.

"Is this it?" Felix said, staring at the innards of the gunship. Besides the cramped cockpit, there had been only a single seat behind each turret.

The pilot turned to them and smiled. "Welcome aboard. This is a Talon-class gunship. I'm afraid a three-person crew is all we can stuff in here. What are your names, privates?"

The woman cleared her throat nervously. "Private Elaine Connors, sir!" she shouted over the heavy roar of the jets.

Felix hadn't been sure how to answer. He'd been given a name. *No.* Assigned a name. The name of his former self, a man whom he'd known nothing about. "Private Felix Amaya, sir." The words sounded strange leaving his mouth. A tinge of guilt weighed on him, like a child telling a lie.

"Welcome aboard, killers. I hope you enjoyed your six-year sleep. You can call me Chief, by the way. Prepare for departure."

"Six-year sleep?" asked Felix.

"Six light years. That's how long it took your data to reach Ruun. Please fasten your safety harnesses."

Felix and Connors sat down and strapped themselves in. Connors took the port gun while he took starboard. Intuitively, he cocked the machine gun and swiveled the turret. First up and down, then side-to-side. He couldn't believe it. Everything was kicking into place, just as Nolan had said it would.

The bay's domed ceiling parted down the middle, both sides retracting open. A slew of aircraft zoomed upward and dispersed into the night.

The Talon fired up and jerked skyward, bouncing them around in their seats. Once the craft leveled out above the bay, the rumbling settled. Now airborne, Felix glimpsed his first look at the colony as it sat nuzzled against the base of the Akkavian mountains. Through the blanket of smoke, he spied the cluster of domes that had made up the base and the barracks where ground transports had already begun to mobilize out the eastern gate. Towards the western sector, a sprawl of large buildings huddled beside the smaller dwellings where he assumed most settlers lived and conducted their day-to-day affairs. A quarry had been dug along its northernmost boundaries, where drilling machines and oil rigs actively excavated deep into the mountain.

The gunship thrust eastward, piercing the smokescreen. There, Ruun greeted him with all its beauty and its terror.

A colossal red moon hung in the northern sky where only the vague silhouettes of majestic mountains painted the horizon.

Southward, swaths of scorched, pockmarked earth marred what would have been an otherwise idyllic valley. The wreckage of downed vehicles smoldered as flames now canvased much of the landscape. As far as the eye could see, stacks of smoke spiraled upward, raining down ash like snowfall.

Gunships fired tracer rounds into the fields of tall grass surrounding the colony. Even along the extreme forward lines, gunfire flashed throughout the prairie, sometimes sporadically beside the crumbled outposts that sat like ancient vestiges.

A warm breeze swept across his face. Below, the tall grass swayed gently in response. Though in the dark he couldn't be sure if the flutter of grass had also been indicative of enemy movement.

"We're on patrol duty so we're cutting away from the main action," Chief said. "You know, just in case those fucks try to flank us along the mountain pass." The Talon banked left, pulling away from the frontlines and accelerated northeast along the mountain range.

Behind them, a company broke into five platoons and fanned outward, the soldiers appearing as specks until the grass consumed them entirely.

The ship decelerated as it flew low and close along the side of a small mountain. Above, the shrubs on the cliffs shifted. Connors pivoted the gun, actively tracking any potential ambush zones alongside the jutting crests and ridges.

"You two been briefed on vamps yet?" Chief asked.

"No," Connors said, before Felix could respond. "They haven't told us shit."

Chief nodded. "Vicious, sneaky, hairless bastards. They're nocturnal on account sunlight blinds them and burns their skin. You know, like vampires from the movies and stuff. They have sharp teeth and little pincer tongues that slurp blood from their prey."

"Where are they?" Felix asked. "I mean their base."

"They don't have one. They live in the mountain caves or the subterranean systems below our feet. It's not like they'd have a base, anyway. They're nomadic. Tribal. I heard not long after humans touched down, they banded together to orchestrate night assaults."

"I'm assuming," Connors said, "they hunt in the tall grass."

"That's right," Chief said. He flipped on a switch. A small monitor beside his right leg powered on. The world appeared in radiant greyscale. Chief turned his head left and the feed picked up what he saw. A group of small, white oblong shapes no bigger than rats scurried away from the Talon and disappeared into a den along the rockface. "Vamps conceal themselves in the grass when they hunt prey. It's also where they stage most of their attacks on the colony, using a combination of spears, bladed weapons, and harpoon guns."

"That doesn't sound too bad," Connors said.

"Yeah, but they outnumber us ten to one," Chief said, grimacing. "They've been chipping away at us for a hundred years, gaining ground, making us burn through our resources and manpower. A goddamn war of attrition."

Felix spared a glimpse at the burning valley. "Why's the world on fire? Always quaking?"

"There are pockets of gas in the caverns below Ruun. Certain plants' roots grow these big pouches that absorb the gasses and spew them up and outward through their stalks, making the air highly combustible."

"Fuck," Felix said. "And why are we at war with the vamps?"

Chief shook his head. "I don't know, Private. I've only been here five days."

Felix leaned back against his seat and pursed his lips. Another carbon copy. He wondered if anyone had been around long enough to know why they were fighting.

The roof of the Talon clanged, as if a storm of marbles had poured down on it. His finger inched near the machine gun's trigger as he swept the turret across his field of view. Sediment spilled over the side of the doors.

Chief ignited the overhead searchlights. Twin purple beams cut across the dark as they searched the slope of the mountain. Through Chief's monitor, Felix saw the lights outline the shape of a cloaked being as it flung itself off a cliff.

"Vamps!" Chief shouted.

Connors quickly swiveled her machine gun skyward and unloaded a torrent of gunfire. A humanoid creature fell, its flesh ripped apart by a supersonic salvo of lead. As it descended, the creature was, for a brief moment, level with Connors. A shot of compressed air erupted from a weapon in its grasp. Before anyone had time to react, a harpoon had punctured Connors's throat, her warm blood splashing over Felix's face and armor.

Connors gurgled as she wrapped both hands around her neck. As the creature plunged, Felix noticed a line of rope attached to the harpoon. While it unspooled, the cord began to grow taut. "Holy fuck," Chief shouted. "Cut the line!"

Felix unclasped the buckles from his seat's harness and unsheathed a knife from his utility belt. He lunged for the rope. Before he had time to sever it, the line jerked violently. Connors's body, securely restrained in place, lurched forward only slightly, the force instead snapping her head clean from her neck.

The woman's headless corpse eased its grip on the machine gun until her hands fell limply at her sides.

A slew of small blasts echoed in the distance. Before Felix could return to his turret, a storm of harpoons struck and bounced off the Talon's canopy, fracturing the windshield. The latticework of broken glass obstructed all visibility.

Numerous thuds hit the roof of the gunship, the weight of their impact denting the roof.

"Shit," Chief cried out. "Suiciders!"

The Talon banked right, shaking loose a cluster of vamps. As it did, a single creature clutched onto the Talon's railings underneath Connors's turret. With a great heave, it quickly vaulted aboard as Chief leveled the craft.

The vamp stood upright and snarled at Felix, revealing its pointed teeth. It was a tall, gangly thing with a pale, sunken face and round orbitals with black pinhole pupils. A single red star-like mark was etched upon its forehead. Its body was draped in dark robes, where a strap looped diagonally around its torso, securing the scimitar at its back.

Felix unslung his rifle and fired off three shots.

The vamp crouched, planted two bony hands on the floor, and sprang out of the way.

Before he could fire again, the creature reached for Chief as he grasped for the controls.

"Can't see a thing. I'm gonna descend-"

The vamp closed both hands around Chief's neck and thrust its mouth into his throat. It dislodged a chunk of flesh and collar bone, causing the gaping wound to cascade dark blood onto the instrumentation panel. The vamp discarded Chief, leaving his head to slam against the throttle.

Felix spun toward the vamp, aimed, and fired a full-auto volley, but the Talon pitched downward, causing him to lose his footing. The shots missed their target, completely eviscerating the cockpit instead.

As the gunship descended into freefall, his body slammed against the back of Chief's seat, knocking the wind from his lungs.

The Talon began to spin and spiral. The vamp hissed as it was launched backward, its body smashing against the tail-end of the ship.

For a moment the two of them locked eyes. Felix wasn't sure if he felt fear or anger then, and he wasn't sure he cared. Survival was the only thing on his mind.

He remembered the cross on the back of his hand and tried to recite a prayer in his head but found he couldn't remember one. Instead, he gripped his rifle and shut his eyes. It was all the religion he could invoke.

They fell for a moment that stretched into eternity, his guts trying desperately to crawl out of his mouth. Then the Talon smashed against the earth, nose-first. His body was tossed back and upward so that he crashed into Connors's torso, his visor shattering. Felix removed his helmet, dropped it, and turned toward the open doorway.

As he stepped forward, his knees buckled, causing him to topple. He tried to stand. Every muscle strained, his body protesting his every movement with scorching pain. He inhaled a deep breath and forced himself to bellycrawl along the floor, his legs slogging along a sea of glass. After a while, he managed to drag himself out of the wreckage.

Once he'd crawled onto the cold, rugged base of the mountain, he noticed the hot, sticky fluid running down his face. He wasn't sure if it was blood or motor oil.

Or both.

Felix closed his eyes. He wanted desperately to sleep and awaken somewhere else, anywhere but this fresh hell. He hated the man who signed the contract that had borne him into a life of servitude to fight a perpetual war against ghouls from another world. He hated the man who got himself into that position to begin with. Surely he'd been a murderer. A gangbanger. Society's trash. Felix laughed. He knew nothing about who he was except that he hated himself.

There came the sound of feet treading over gravel. He snapped his eyes open and rolled over onto his back. Not far from him, a shadow began to stir. Its gait was that of a wounded creature, but it hobbled forward nonetheless. A glint of red moonlight caught on the vamp's body, illuminating the shredded rags hanging from its figure.

It drew its sword.

Eyes raging and teeth bared, it came for Felix.

The creature took a long single bound, landed two meters in front of Felix, and drew its arm back. The scimitar glimmered as it hung in the moonlight.

The curved blade came down on his head. Felix grasped his rifle, shoving it upward with both hands. His weapon caught the blow just in time. He chambered a kick and thrust it into the vamps left kneecap. The pop of cracking bone—much like the sound of splintering wood—reverberated off the side of the mountain.

The creature collapsed, shrieking like a bat.

Suddenly the earth trembled.

Felix pushed off the quaking ground and jabbed the butt of his rifle into the vamp's temple.

A thousand cracks formed in the ground around the downed gunship, encompassing them in a web of fractured terrain.

The vamp hissed and dug a set of sharp nails into Felix's shin. With its other hand it raised its sword once again.

Felix clamped his teeth and pointed the barrel of his rifle at the creature's face.

Before either combatant could execute a killing blow, the earth collapsed beneath them, plunging their bodies into a dark abyss.

He opened his eyes and there was darkness. He knew only that he was in excruciating pain and that he no longer held his rifle. A hiss echoed somewhere in the dark, telling him that he'd been in the belly of some spacious subterranean cavern. The sound of footsteps approached. Blindly, he probed the ground for his weapon.

Nothing.

He quickly patted his combat armor, his fingers sliding past a medkit and some ammo pouches. Then he found what he'd been looking for. He snapped the flare and watched as it sparked alive.

There was no sign of the vamp.

He struggled to his feet and looked around. The chamber was indeed spacious, being almost as wide as the hangar at east bay.

His boots crunched over rust-colored sediment. Along the cave walls, the stalks of peculiar fungi swayed to a draft of hot air. Above, flesh-like bags dangled from the ceiling, thick strands of roots springing from their underbellies like coarse hair.

Strangest of all, the bags pulsed like lungs.

He gently lowered his flare, bringing it close to his chest. He was lucky he hadn't blown up yet. Perhaps the opening had released most of the gasses, or maybe the roots had filtered them out all already.

Up ahead, the light from the flare glimmered on the surface of a metallic construct. He unholstered his pistol and stepped forward.

The object appeared to be a winged vessel about the same size as the carrier ships he'd seen, but its shape and design couldn't have been more alien. It was almost asymmetrical, even curved and rounded in certain areas where aircraft had no business being curved and rounded. A ramp led into the mouth of the ship. He shoved the flare in front of his body as he ascended the slope.

Gelatinous membranes clung to the walls of the craft, like the tissue surrounding the inner lining of a stomach. In the dark, leaning against what resembled a cockpit, a tangle of jagged, thorny legs enveloped a hideous thing as it slumbered. He knew the thing was sleeping because its shape rose and fell gently as if it were breathing. The flare began to die. He stepped back. The reverberation of his footfalls caused the membrane walls to vibrate until they retracted like slime, slithering into what appeared to be the monster's head.

Felix felt a cold hand wrap around his neck, followed quickly by a burning sting on his throat. He spun around. The vamp stepped back, a trickle of blood on its lips. It scowled as it eased its grip on its sword.

A fire spread through Felix's veins, his skin feeling like it had been doused in flames. He fell to his knees and clutched his face. Like water merging with oil, strange vivid colors filled his vision.

Synaptic bursts fired in his head, scrambling the world around him. Fragmented images began to filter through his brain, like a pirated television broadcast.

Then in rapid succession the images came:

In the sunlight, he saw glimmering cities extending across familiar swaths of tall grass. A distinct people of dark complexion basking in the night air beneath a red moon.

He bore witness to hideous crab-like creatures emerging from the depths, their hordes overwhelming entire armies, tearing soldiers apart with pointed pincers. Their thorny exoskeletons housing a mass of squirming protean brains. Krikirak! Krikirak! is the noise they made as they fed.

Another vision. Droves of people abandoning their great cities as they fled into the darkest of caves, where the krikiraks slept but could not see.

Countless revolutions passed and, in the night, a new race emerged from the womb of evolution: a race born to see in the dark, hunting quietly by night, wary of the long dormant krikiraks and their cyclical feasts.

Then he observed countless vessels descending from the sky like falling stars. A colony anchoring itself along the mountains.

Great drilling machines and oil derricks pierced the earth, slowly rattling the beasts early from their slumber.

Finally, war. Night after night, waves of bodies slamming into the colony walls in attempts to silence the quaking and the fire, in efforts to save native and colonizer alike.

Felix regurgitated bile onto the ground.

The vamp watched him, unmoving, making no attempt to execute him. Felix stood and inhaled a deep breath. His eyes had adjusted considerably well in the dark as he could now see the vamp clearly before him.

What was happening to him?

They locked eyes once again. The vamp nodded, its eyes now having lost all their rage.

He remembered then. The inoculations. It would take a few days for the stuff to work.

He was slowly turning into one of them.

Felix understood then. At least he thought he did. Humans thought the bites carried disease and caused hallucinations, but that couldn't be further from the truth. Since the time the vamps had abandoned all ties to their technology, they had somehow evolved. Some mutation that allowed for the transfer of genetic information, of their history, all through their saliva. Records, stories, information. All things cultures had passed down and valued above all else.

Felix nodded back. He wasn't sure where they'd go from here, but for the moment, they faced a bigger threat than themselves.

"Thank you for not killing me," Felix whispered. He patted his chest. "My name is... Felix."

The vamp bowed its head slightly, understanding the gesture. It formed an undecipherable string of clicks using its teeth.

"I can't pronounce that," he said, pursing his lips. His thoughts dwelled suddenly on Connors. The baby on her arm. He didn't want to think of the vamp as a thing, a creature. He was an individual with fears and wants. He would give him a nickname. At least until he could learn to pronounce his real name. "How about I call you Curtis for now?"

The vamp tilted his head and shrugged in confusion.

There came the clamber of furious scuttling. At their backs the krikirak emerged from the tail of the ancient vamp ship. It was large, like some primordial insect from Earth's past. A set of six thorny crimson legs carried a round, flat carapace. Its head consisted of a pair of insectoid-like eyes on either side of a porous skull, which contained its slithering, gooey brain. At the tip of the skull were two razor-sharp pincers, longer, even, than Curtis's scimitars.

The creature lunged, snapping its pincers together. Its mouth ejected a long tongue embedded with needlelike barbs. As its mouth writhed, it formed a shrill shriek. "Krikirak! Krikirak!"

Curtis shoved Felix out of the way and brought his sword down on a spiny leg. Its shell deflected the blow. The krikirak swung a leg, knocking Curtis sideways.

Felix took two quick steps back and emptied his clip into the creature's carapace. Besides a few minor cracks, its armor held.

"Fuck," he said, reloading.

The krikirak screeched and scurried, swinging its forelegs like feelers. He had almost forgotten the thing was blind in the dark. Yet still it came. His back almost pressed against solid stone; there had been nowhere to go beside the downed Talon. The hole in the earth was too far up to climb out of. Felix grimaced as he took aim.

Before the creature could strike, Curtis hobbled in from its left flank and springboarded off a single leg. He brought his sword down on its skull, the blade striking a piece of exposed brain. The monster shrieked, the sound like steel scraping against steel.

The creature's malleable brain swirled around the sword and slithered toward another crevice in its skull. Curtis clasped the scimitar and heaved, but the blade had lodged itself into solid bone.

A pair of legs shot from the krikirak's side and reached for the vamp.

A translucent sac of gelatinous orbs shifted under the creature's carapace. The thing was pregnant.

"Fuck!" Felix shouted. His mind raced. A pointed leg swung at Curtis, the vamp just barely ducking out of the way. An idea came. Felix drew a flare from a pouch. "Hey," he called, swinging his arms. He lit the flare.

Curtis turned, his hands shielding his eyes from the brightness.

"Catch!" Felix lobbed the flare. The vamp caught it, closed his eyes, and jabbed the burning end into the monster's head.

A loud roar bellowed from the spasming beast. It bucked Curtis from its carapace. As Curtis lay on the floor, the krikirak treaded over his body, its legs piercing his abdomen.

As it flailed in agony, Felix swooped beside Curtis and dragged him toward the downed gunship.

Blood now poured freely from Curtis' wounds. Viscera began to seep from his gashes. Curtis clacked his teeth, though Felix wasn't sure if he was speaking or simply chattering from the pain.

Felix eyed the broken turrets and cursed under his breath.

The krikirak regained itself and rotated in the dark, its legs feeling about the air madly.

As he held Curtis, Felix looked up. The chasm that swallowed them whole was large, and he could still see the world beyond it;

gentle, swaying shrubs, the mountain face, the glimmer of red moonlight.

The krikirak's tongue slid along the floor until it came upon a trail of blood. It clicked its pincers and followed the gory path.

In the distance, the sound of bombs reverberated across the air. Sediment rained down from the cavern's ceiling, coating the world in dust.

Then, an idea. He only hoped that it would work. He settled Curtis gently on the floor and reached for his helmet. He secured it on his head and flipped a switch. The visor had shattered but some of its features still worked. The HUD powered on. He blinked and toggled through a list of functions. Then he found what he was looking for.

Airstrike Targeting.

As the krikirak neared the Talon, Felix's broken display outlined its frame in a flashing red outline. The computer system prompted a series of warnings, which he quickly dismissed. The helmet's internal positioning system immediately beamed its coordinates to Alpha, which would in turn triangulate back to Sarkov's Landing.

The monster clicked its pincers and screeched in triumph as it lifted its charred head and pounded its legs on the floor like a war drum.

It had detected them.

Felix smiled. The unmistakable roar of an approaching craft neared as it ripped through the sky.

He lifted Curtis, who had now been spewing blood from his mouth, and cradled him as his breaths became weaker. The vamp clutched Felix's hand and offered a final squeeze.

The krikirak charged, its eggs quivering under its frame.

Above, a gliding shadow draped over them. Then came a piercing whistle.

Before the bombs detonated, Felix hoped that the war would come to an end. He'd only known it for a night, but its terrors were enough to last a lifetime.

But he had played his part, and that's what mattered.

He sighed and made peace with his past. He wasn't sure what the future held, but for once, he felt hopeful, knowing now that with every rebirth, Man and Woman were offered a new chance to make things right.

The krikirak jabbed its pincers into his flesh.

In a flash of brilliance, fire engulfed the world, and before darkness took him, he had at long last known who he was.

Do as I Do

Maria dipped a single hand into the cool silver stream and cupped it into the form of a saucer. "Now, do as I do," she said to the robot staring blankly at her. It put down the assault rifle and dipped its hand into the running liquid. Its metal hand closed and imitated her as best as it could.

She lifted her hand, now holding a small amount of water. "Go on, try it."

The robot lifted its hand and water spilled through its fingers.

"No, no. Try it again. You have to learn. It's important."

The robot plunged its hand into the water again. Its digits shut together and formed a curved hand. It raised its hand and looked at Maria. She lowered her head and saw the small puddle of water. "Yes, that's good."

She raised her cupped hand close to her chest, where she cradled a puppy no older than a few days. The pup's mouth opened, making sucking motions as it whimpered. She angled her hand so that its mouth suckled on the edge of her palm. She tipped her hand slightly and water trickled into the pup's mouth.

Maria nodded at the robot. The robot held a pup who stared at it with closed eyes and a protruding mouth. The robot tilted its hand and water spilled onto the puppy's face. The small creature squirmed and shook in the robot's grasp.

"No, you have to be gentle, or you'll drown it. You understand me? It'll die. Your motions have to be slow and graceful."

The robot stared at her dumbly. "Graceful?" it said in a voice that sounded like metal scraping against metal.

"Yes. Delicate. Tip your hand slowly so that only a trickle escapes your palm. Try again."

The robot cupped a handful of water and lowered it to the puppy's mouth. Maria watched with a subdued breath. It had been difficult trusting a machine. She remembered when it happened so many years ago. She was just a girl then. The news reporters said some sort of corrupt programming had caused the world's military machines to turn on all living things. They said their infrared sensors had become faulty and began targeting anything with a heat signature. That meant most living creatures on Earth. But by the time the world had figured out what was wrong, the machines had begun constructing their own children, passing on their source code along with all their faulty programming. They were so resourceful. But Maria knew nothing of science or even of the technology that had made her television work. All she knew was the fear that drove her. It had been months since she had seen another survivor. That's what made this so important.

She looked up. The sun started to cross the hills to the west. In about two hours it would be dark. She turned her attention to the robot. It lowered its hand slower this time. A steady palm tilted downward, and a trickle of clear water funneled into the puppy's mouth. The puppy gleefully drank it up.

"That's good. See? You can do it."

The robot regarded her for a moment, nodded, and then returned its focus to the pup. There was hope for the robot yet.

"All right, we have to move now. It's going to be dark, and our heat signature will stand out like a sore thumb. Give me the puppy."

"I do not emit heat, Ms. Maria."

"I meant me and the puppies."

"I see. I am sorry."

The robot extended its hand and Maria took the puppy from its grasp. She put both of their naked bodies into her backpack and zipped it nearly shut, allowing just enough of a gap to let some air in. Their muffled whines broke her heart, and she tried to ignore them until they could find a place to sleep. She slung the AK-47 toward her chest and brushed off trace amounts of dust from the barrel.

"Will we be returning to the cave again this evening?" the robot asked, retrieving its own Kalashnikov.

"No. We have to keep moving south. We need to find survivors."

"Statistically, there may be more survivors north, in the US."

"No, no. That was the source of all of this. There is less technology down south. I heard there is an elaborate cave system in

Oaxaca with an underwater lake. We could live there, and they wouldn't be able to detect our heat signatures from above. If we move fast enough, we can reach it in about a week."

"Have you been there?" asked the robot.

"No, I've never seen too much of the countryside. I know that they lived in poverty and that technology was scarce in that part of Mexico. The government always seemed to disregard those people and their requests for modernization. Now it's the only thing that may have staved off total annihilation." She sighed. "Why am I even telling you all this? You're just a dumb robot."

The robot said nothing and looked away.

Maria filled her canteen and strapped on her backpack. The extra weight from the provisions and the puppies made her back pain flare up again. She suppressed a moan and walked forward. The terrain on the slope of the hill was rocky and uneven. As she walked, she felt the sharp pebbles stab through her soles and jab at her feet. In short time she would need new shoes. *Just ignore it,* she told herself. She wanted to climb to a higher elevation to get a better grasp of her surroundings. She knew, though, that the robots had utilized smart drones in the air. It was a calculated risk.

The robot slipped a few times but readjusted itself. Its hands probed and pulled on rocky fissures and footholds as it clambered behind her. It wasn't designed for any outdoor trekking; it was a city robot made for city jobs. It had been a prototype protocol model on display at the Mexico City Technological Exhibit when the world went to hell. The robot was marketed as a maid for the wealthy.

Maria had found it a week ago under the rubble of the convention building, pinned against a construction beam. For all she knew it had been pinned there for years. At first she thought it was a person, and she pulled and heaved, trying so desperately to save its life. When the beam came loose, she reeled in horror.

It had hobbled toward her and thanked her. Its right leg had sustained damage. It said it was at her service. She didn't know what to do. Ultimately, she had thought the robot stupid and only good for menial tasks and small talk. She decided to take it with her even though she didn't quite trust it. It seemed harmless enough, and it wasn't a military robot. And after Isidro, the robot was her first real companion. She had laughed hysterically at the irony before the tears came.

After a few minutes of hiking up the hill, the puppies stopped whining. She knew her legs were going to be sore. They already felt heavy, like they were dipped in drying cement.

As she reached the top of the hill, she took off the backpack and paused for a breath. She arched her back and felt the pain kick in again. The robot reached the top and stared blankly ahead. They had a panoramic view to the south. Plain green fields and small hills rolled as far as the horizon. The sky was clear and violet, and a cool breeze swept in. Maria closed her eyes and thought about Isidro. She had only known him for a few days before she lost him, but he had filled that time with more life than all her nineteen years of living.

She turned north. Off in the far distance were the ruins of Mexico City. Skyscrapers sat broken and jagged, and the urban sprawl lay deserted. She had spent years there, scurrying like a rat, avoiding the onslaught of robot scouts who picked off the last survivors of civilization. One by one everyone she knew had succumbed to starvation, disease, or mechanized murder. That's when she decided to leave.

The sun sank below the western horizon. The day's last light would be snuffed out before long.

"Come on. Let's go." She reached for the backpack, but the robot had already strapped it to its back. "Thank you, Robot," she said.

"You are welcome, Ms. Maria."

"Just call me Maria. I suppose I should give you a name, I'm getting tired of calling you Robot all the time. What would you like to be called?"

"I do not understand, Maria."

"Pick a name for yourself, something that describes you." She forced a smile in an attempt at warmth.

"I understand. I am Robot."

Maria sighed and shook her head. Below, the unknown awaited. She gripped the rifle tight against her chest. She descended the southern edge of the hill.

"Come on, let's go, Robot."

"Now, do as I do," Maria said, as she opened a small can of beans.

Robot pulled back the lid of his tin can. His other hand slightly crushed the sides of the can. He was trying to be as gentle as possible.

It had been two days since she had taught Robot to cup water from a stream. Since then, she had let him help with other small tasks like bathing the puppies and checking them for fleas and wounds. She'd found them amidst a dead litter on the outskirts of Mexico City. The mother was nowhere to be found, and Maria had to assume that she had been eaten by some wild animal. She took pity on the surviving puppies and decided there was enough room for them in her backpack.

Maria retrieved a spoon and handed it to Robot. She made sure he was looking before taking her spoon and mashing the beans together into a smooth pulp. She picked up one of the puppies and cradled it on her lap as she sat on the floor against a tree.

"When they're young they don't have teeth, so they need to ingest something smooth. You understand?"

Robot nodded. "Yes, Maria. I understand."

"And we won't have beans forever. You can mash berries into pulp, too."

She brought the spoon to the puppy's mouth. Its mouth jutted out and a small tongue lapped up the bean paste. Maria looked at Robot.

Robot mashed up the beans inside his can and pulled out the spoon. Inside the can was a smooth brown paste. He held the puppy in one hand and fed it with the other just as she had showed him.

"That's good, Robot. You're learning."

"I am pleased to serve you."

"You serve them, Robot. We have to take care of them. All life is precious, and we need to make sure no harm comes to them. We have to stick together."

"Like a family?" asked Robot.

"Yes, like a family."

A sharp pain twisted in her insides, and she leaned across the tree. She regurgitated the water she had drunk that morning. Her guts felt like spilling out her throat as she spewed her lunch onto a patch of grass. The feeling had been getting more frequent. Her abdominal muscles were contracting violently now.

"Is everything all right, Maria?" Robot asked.

"Yes, I'm fine, Robot. Must've been a bad batch of water." She leaned against the tree and closed her eyes.

"Very well. Would you like to take the puppy back?"

"The puppy? Oh, yes." She had a thought. "Robot, would you like to name one of the puppies?"

Robot stared at her blankly.

"Go on. Just like you named yourself. Mine's a boy, I'll name him Roberto, like my father."

Robot stared at the puppy in silence.

"You have a girl puppy. Go ahead and name her."

"I will name her Robot Junior."

Maria gritted her teeth. She fought the urge to scream, took a breath, and said, "You don't quite get how the name thing works, do you? That's not exactly a girl's name."

"Why?" asked Robot.

She opened her mouth to explain the differences between male and female names, and stopped herself. It would take too long. "Never mind. You win. She can be Robot Junior."

Robot held Robot Jr. in his hands and nodded. He gave her back to Maria.

She placed Roberto and Robot Jr. in her bag and finished the rest of the bean paste in silence.

Robot stood upright and stared off into the distance. She wondered if he could think like she could. What kind of thoughts ran through his head?

"What are you thinking about, Robot?"

"I do not think, Maria. I only react to my environment. Abstract thought, hindsight, foresight: I am incapable of such things."

Maria nodded. She was placing all her trust in him. It was crazy. Maybe she had gone mad.

"Robot, how long do you have to live?"

"I am afraid that question does not apply to me. I am not alive. My battery cell has another thirty years left of charge, if that is what you refer to."

"I see. So, Robot, you've never felt alive?"

"I cannot answer that question. Is there anything else I may assist you with?"

Maria sighed and bit her lip. "No. Let's get a move on. Oaxaca is a couple of days away. We've been lucky avoiding the other robots so far. After this point we'll be walking through open fields, and we'll be more easily spotted. Once in Oaxaca, we'll be near the jungle."

"As you wish, Maria."

As she stood, her stomach ached. Her muscles felt like knots. She put a hand on her stomach and her belly felt warm.

She walked out from the cool shade of the tree. Her face felt flushed as the open sun beat down on her.

As she turned, Robot strapped the backpack on before she could get to it. He limped to her side and awaited her command. She patted his shoulder and said, "All right, let's move."

— ⁓ —

The sky boomed with the sound of jet thrusters. Maria knew the familiar sound of the drones. She sprinted as fast as her aching legs would let her. Robot hobbled behind her, the whine of puppies at his back. If they even got a read on her heat signature it would be over. She knew the protocol: the drones would alert the others, and they would deploy ground units to verify the liquidation of the target. If the drone missiles didn't get her first. It would be over only when the target was acquired and destroyed.

The trees were thick and tall and thin slivers of sunlight pierced the canopy like spears. She had no time to focus on the dense, sticky air of the humid jungle. Leaves and palms slapped her face as she jumped over vines and barbs.

Sweat trickled in her eyes. She stopped to rub them and catch her breath. The drones hovered above her position. She couldn't see anything above the veil of trees. Had they detected her? A small stream ran under her feet. Just a trickle, but the water forged a small path through the jungle floor. In the distance she heard a dull roar, like static on a radio.

Maria looked at Robot and pointed in the direction of the sound. They jogged forward. A few miles deep into the stream the air became cooler, and the sound grew louder. The stream widened into a small river, its current growing rapid and violent.

Ahead, the river ran off a rocky ledge. Mists of water shot upward, and Maria could see small rainbows materializing in the air. The line of trees ended here, and the sky opened up above.

"That must be it," she whispered to Robot under the shade of a tree. "The waterfall leads to the underground caves. If we can get down there, we could hide and live off the land."

Robot nodded as he surveyed the sky. "We will be exposed," he said, pointing at the empty sky above. "The descent would allow the drones to target us easily."

Maria kneeled on the ground. Her insides churned. She groaned and leaned an arm against a tree.

"What is the matter?" asked Robot.

"We have to get to the caves. No matter what."

Robot slung his rifle behind his torso and placed an arm on her shoulder.

The air burst with fire and cracked with the sound of thunder. It sounded like the sky was tearing apart.

Behind them, a half a mile to their north, the trees caught fire and swayed savagely.

Another explosion lit the trees a few hundred feet from their position.

"They know I'm here," Maria shouted.

Robot swept Maria off the ground and cradled her in his arms. He hobbled along the river as fast as he could. Another explosion decimated the tree where they had just stood. Robot crossed the end of the tree line as he ran exposed under the clear sky. He heard the hum of a drone overhead but didn't stop to look. Robot ran to the edge of the cliff and jumped. Another eruption echoed at the edge of the cliff as he saw the cascade of white water fall into a wide lake below.

Together, the woman, the robot, and the puppies plunged into the cool pool of water.

Robot released Maria from his grip. She swam for the surface. He unshouldered the backpack and raised his arms upward as his feet pedaled swiftly. Two hands plunged into the water and took the bag from his grasp.

He breached the surface of the water and saw Maria quickly opening the backpack on a small, rocky shore. Behind her was the small oval opening to a cave where the water streamed briskly through. Robot pulled himself onto a flat rock, where Maria pulled out the still bodies of the puppies.

"What is their status?"

"They're not breathing."

Maria laid the small body of Roberto flat on the rock and pressed her lips to his. She blew into his mouth and pushed her hands against his chest. "Robot, do as I do."

Robot cradled Robot Jr. in his hands and placed her gently on the rock. "I am incapable of breathing life into her."

"Press against her chest. The pressure should cause her to spit out the water."

Robot pressed against Robot Jr.'s chest with his palm. Her small paws hung limp and lifeless at her sides. He looked back at Maria. Roberto coughed up water and began moving his head. His eyes opened for the first time and he let out a small whine. Robot looked back at Robot Jr. He pressed at her chest with his finger. He pressed again. And again.

"Please breathe, Robot Junior."

He lightly caressed the puppy's face with his finger. Her mouth opened. Robot pressed her chest again, rhythmically now. Water spewed down the side of her small muzzle. She opened her eyes and whined.

Maria picked up Roberto and touched Robot's shoulder. "You did it, Robot. You just saved all our lives." Tears streamed down her cheeks.

"I am pleased to serve you all. Shall we go inside now, Maria?"

She wiped the tears from her face and nodded. "Yes, let's take a look inside."

Robot carried the pup. She squirmed in his hands as her eyes darted at the world around her.

They crouched through the mouth of the cave. Inside, a dark, open, humid world welcomed them. A few beams of sunlight pierced the dark ceiling above, lighting the space around them. The stream of water ran through multiple passageways. At the nexus of the cave was a large spacious area lined with moss and craggy walls.

Maria picked a path and trudged forward. The path led through a tight, winding trail. Maria brought Roberto against her chest and squeezed through bumpy cave walls. Robot did the same with his pup as his back scraped against rock.

They found themselves in another spacious chamber where much of the stream collected into a small lake. Maria handed her pup to Robot and grimaced. She sat on a large, flat rock and held her belly. She moaned and her cries echoed through the cavernous chamber.

"What is the matter, Maria?"

"It's time, Robot. I'm having a baby. My water just broke."

"I am confused. You are pregnant?"

"Haven't you noticed? My belly? My aches? My vomiting?"

"I know little about human biology. How may I help?"

"Just stay with me," she said as she rested against a craggy wall.

Robot sat beside her and placed the puppies down. They tried to walk but toppled over their clumsy legs. After a while they fell asleep at his side.

Maria reached over the rock and cupped a hand of water and drank.

"Why did you not inform me of your condition?" Robot asked.

"You have to understand, Robot, I don't know how many survivors are out there. I didn't want anyone knowing I harbor life inside me. The risks were too high. And, well, you're a robot."

Robot said nothing as he stared at the slumbering pups.

Maria placed a hand on Robot's shoulder. "But now I know you're a friend."

A sharp pain pulsed inside Maria's gut. She held on to Robot's arm and squeezed. She lay on the ground and removed her pants. She closed her eyes.

"I'm in pain, Robot."

"Tell me about the male who impregnated you."

Maria stared at Robot and then nodded.

"His name was Isidro. He was a little older than me. He was the only survivor I had seen in over a year. At least it feels like it was over a year. He was nice. He taught me how to use the rifles. I don't know any more about him," she moaned.

"Stay focused. Please tell me more."

She screamed at the cave ceiling. "He had darker skin than me and had beautiful brown eyes. Told me his family was killed by robots when he was fifteen years old. He had been hiding in the subway station, sleeping on the rails. He had to come out of hiding because food was running short. That's when I met him. I was scavenging an old pet store for food. It had been looted long ago, but there he was, frightened and joyous all at once. Like me."

Robot moved his hand to hers and clamped it gently shut. She squeezed as her moans roared down the cavern.

"We were only together a few days before we were separated. A drone spotted us from above and fired on our position. He told me it would be best to split up. The drone chased him while I ran the opposite way. My mother would've liked him."

Maria broke into a heavy sweat and spread her legs. As she screamed, Robot watched as a small head appeared from under her.

"Catch the baby before it hits the ground."

A body slid out and Robot extended his hands. The baby took the shape of a small, wet human. Robot held it in his hands and pulled it completely out.

"There is a hose attached to this child," Robot said as he delivered the baby to Maria. She cradled the baby in her arms as it cried with small, outstretched hands.

"It's an umbilical cord. Find me a sharp-edged rock."

Robot looked on the cave floor and found nothing that suited. He slammed a fist against the wall and a few pieces of rock broke loose. He found the sharpest one and handed it to Maria. She severed the cord. She squeezed the baby to her chest. It was like nothing she could ever describe. All she knew was peace.

"It's a beautiful baby boy, Robot." Maria smiled.

Robot nodded and stared in what Maria assumed was curiosity.

She extended her arms and said, "Hold him."

Robot held out an open hand.

"No. Do as I do," she said. Maria cradled the baby with both arms against her chest and rocked him side to side.

Robot took the baby and did as Maria instructed. He cradled the child and rocked him side to side. The baby stared at the robot for a while and closed his eyes.

A sound boomed in the distance. The echoes of hums and loud footsteps filled the cave.

"They are here," Maria said.

"We must go," Robot said, slinging his rifle around with one free hand.

"No. They already know I'm here. They'll keep hunting until they've found me. Then they'll discover all of us."

Robot stood quiet and stared into the darkness.

"I think you understand, Robot. This is goodbye."

"I am confused. I do not know what to do."

Maria hobbled back toward the cave entrance and turned to Robot. Her shoes were tattered, and her clothes bloodied. "Just do as I did." She smiled, cocked her rifle, and brought it up to her bosom. With that she vanished into the dark and toward the raging rapids of the waterfall.

For a while there was silence. Robot looked at the baby and crouched by the lake. He dipped his hand into the blue waters and scrubbed some of the blood off the baby's face. "I will name you Isidro," Robot said, and softly tapped the baby's nose.

He turned to the puppies, sleeping on the rock, and sat beside them with Isidro in his arms.

A loud burst thundered through the caves, the unmistakable sound of machine-gun fire. Then silence once more.

He looked at the pups and the baby. Their sleeping bodies, still and peaceful.

Beyond the cave was a world of death. But in the cave, he was sure of one thing: there was life.

"Do not worry. I will be here," he said, looking at the three small lives around him. "Perhaps we can look for more family."

As day fell and the sunlight faded from the ceiling above, Robot stared into the dark and waited for his children's hungry cries.

Sneeze

As Rogelio woke that winter morning, Grandpa Ludovico stepped through the door, his shoulders hunched forward as he sniffled and wiped snot from his nose. He'd returned home early from his morning shift at the sawmill, looking worse than usual. He moaned and slogged his way toward the dining table, his eyes accumulating a thin layer of moisture like a child about to cry.

"Good morning, Mijo," he said, nestling into his seat. He rubbed his eyes and let out a deep sigh.

"Good morning, Abuelito," Rogelio said, smiling. He approached the table and sat beside his grandfather. The man smelled of sweat, coffee, sawdust, and all the scents that came with manhood. "How was work today, Abuelito?"

"Besides having this terrible cold, it was fine," he said. "We cleared a few more acres from the forest. And we were able to finally scatter that tribe from their grounds. They'd been holding up production for months. We had no choice. You know how bad the gringos want our lumber exports. Anyway, the foreman says at the rate we're clearing the trees, we're sure to make our bonuses by the end of the year." His grandfather rubbed his thumb and index finger together as he smiled and said, "Mas lana. More money. Soon I'll be able to retire in comfort. Hell, we'll all be able to take a little vacation."

"Oh, how wonderful," Grandma Clara said, coming out of the kitchen as she held a tray containing two bowls of chicken soup. "The developers will be so happy. This is going to be our year, I just know it."

Grandpa Ludovico winked at her and nodded. "As soon as I get better, I'll be back on those bulldozers in no time instead of barking at those foolish youngbloods. They couldn't fell a tree if—" Suddenly, the man's old face contorted while he fought off an oncoming sneeze.

Grandma Clara set down the steaming bowls of soup beside Grandpa Ludovico and squeezed her husband's shoulder, rocking it gently.

"Ludovico, try to hold it in," Grandma Clara pleaded. She gripped her rosary, bowed her head, and uttered a prayer under her breath.

"I can't fight it anymore," Grandpa Ludovico said, worry in his tone. He shut his eyes and titled his head back.

"What is it, Grandpa?" Rogelio asked jumping out of his chair.

"Mijo," Grandpa Ludovico said, crinkling his nose, "it's time you knew the truth. Every time we sneeze, we create an entire universe. Every speck of spit and snot houses a galaxy, and in seconds, entire life cycles go by, until the mist dissipates, and then—"

"Achooo!" Grandpa Ludovico finally sneezed, shooting a violent spray of moisture and phlegm into the air like a geyser.

"Look, Mijo," he said pointing at the cluster of haze spiraling over the table. The mist swirled and expanded. The specks of moisture hung on a beam of sunlight emanating from the kitchen window. "That's a whole world you're witnessing. You see, time is relative to everything. Even now as we speak life has probably evolved somewhere in there. And now," he said with a bit of excitement, "some species may very well be travelling along the drops, exploring the entirety of their creation. Isn't it wonderful?"

The cluster began to slow its expansion. The droplets scattered in the wind and settled gently on the table and floor. A few droplets landed on Grandpa Ludovico's arm and evaporated instantly on his wrinkled skin.

"We get older and sicker," Grandpa Ludovico said solemnly at the dissolving mist. He hung his head and removed his hardhat, placing it over his heart. "I've destroyed so very much over the years. How many civilizations have I annihilated? Impossible to say."

Rogelio didn't know what to say or do to comfort his grandfather. It was all so much information to take in. He felt like he'd stumbled upon some ancient truth kept secret from mortal ears. It was both wonderful and terrifying at the same time. "Bless you, Abuelito," Rogelio mustered warmly at last, resting a hand on the man's shoulder and squeezing it as his grandmother had. It was all he could offer his grandfather, and he hoped it would be enough.

"Thank you," said Grandpa Ludovico with a warm smile. Then his brows furrowed as he regarded the moisture on the table with eyes of contempt. "Now get me a handkerchief. What a damn mess."

As Rogelio turned to reach for a box of tissue, the wallpaper began to peel into tiny flakes as they scattered in the air like ashes. Then the wood on the wall dissolved in a storm of millions of individual particles. Then came the roof, and the floor, and his hands, and his grandparents, until darkness at last settled neatly into all the empty spaces that had been their world.

Portals to the Past

His sixth birthday. He sat in the park when a swirly rainbow-colored portal opened, like puddles of water and oil. A man appeared.

"Michael, I brought a gift."

"Who are you?"

"Your father Thomas, before he died; traveling from the past."

Thomas offered a red balloon.

"You knew? These are a hundred dollars."

"Helium is scarce by 2031, yes. A gift from the past. Happy birthday."

Thomas faced the portal.

"Are you coming back?"

"Memories are portals to the past. Remember me. I'll always be there."

Thomas winked and vanished.

Michael smiled. The future, like the balloon, never looked so bright.

The *Seeds* of Foundation

Theo walked in the building and felt a little embarrassed. It was a clean, immaculate room with white tile floors and chrome walls. He wore his cleanest white shirt and only pair of slacks. He had polished his shoes shortly before coming. Working construction, he never really needed to look presentable, but today was different.

The room was full of professional men and women speaking into earpieces or at their desks, face-to-face with a customer. A man in a perfectly pressed suit approached him with an even more presentable smile. Theo extended his hand, "Hi, I'm Theo Martinez. I called earlier."

"Ah, yes," the suited man said. "I'm Michael Braun. I spoke to you. Let's walk to my office where we can speak privately."

They walked past offices with people carrying on whispered conversations. A muted television set played a news segment about the second wave of explorers arriving on Mars. They came to a room in the back. Michael Braun bowed his head and waved his hand at the door. Theo entered and sat down.

"Now, Mr. Martinez, we can speak."

A framed picture of Braun's family stared back at Theo: two girls no older than five and a wife with a smile as attractive as her husband's.

"My father came to this country," Theo sighed, "when borders were more than walls on a line. They were a game of Russian roulette. If you didn't die in the desert, or drown crossing the river, you were jumped by drug traffickers or shot by angry ranchers."

Braun reached for a manila folder that read *Burial Services* on it, probably having heard the same story time and time again.

Theo continued. "He raised me in this country alone. My mother left us before I was old enough to remember her face. He did everything to ensure I had a stable living condition. If I didn't achieve success in school, it's only because of my failures, not his as a father." He looked down and took a breath. "He is getting old now."

Braun pressed his lips together and nodded his head, the universal display of 'Yes, I understand.'

"But the worst thing is, Mr. Braun, that he doesn't remember who I am."

Braun looked confused.

"He has Alzheimer's. My creator doesn't recognize his only creation." Theo's eyes became moist. He took a deep breath and forced a smile. "Anyway, I wanted to be ready and give him a proper send-off when the time came."

"Of course," said Braun. He opened the manila folder. "And we have a slew of great options based on your... financial circumstances. Now, our burials are–"

"I don't want him buried, Mr. Braun. Not exactly."

"I see. We do offer cremation services, and they are in fact not as costly."

"No, I was thinking something a little closer to my heart. My father was a gardener, you see; it was the only job he could get here without papers. He would make other people's lawns look perfect, only to come home to a busted-up backhouse. He had huge concrete hands, but he was always so delicate with flowers. Then I heard about the Rebirth Program. It's perfect: a service that sends loved ones to Mars with an assortment of seeds in a bio-degradable coffin, a little something to speed up the terraforming going on there."

"Mr. Martinez, the Rebirth Program has a very steep price tag. And a rather long waiting list."

"I don't have a family," Theo said picking up Braun's family portrait. "I've been saving up just for this. It's the least I can do. He crossed borders to sow the seeds of my foundation. I think it's only proper that he continues doing the same for future generations."

Braun nodded and put the manila folder back. He rifled through his drawer and retrieved a red folder. "Go home and read over these files and bring them back to me signed, and we can begin the process of shipping procedures, coffin selection, and if you'd like to pick a flower arrangement..."

Theo got up and shook Braun's hand. "He is the flowers."

"You really love your father," said Braun.

"And I always will," said Theo. "He's the best dad in the whole world."

The Tailor of Worlds

Carbajal sprinted past the maze of corridors and into the bridge as the hull of the generation ship *Metzlixochitl* creaked and groaned like the whales he'd heard on those ancient audio logs from Earth.

Captain Garcia had been hovering over an instrument panel, his hands gliding over an array of switches and throttles. "Carbajal," he shouted, "what's the status of the cryo chambers?"

"Life systems still operational," he said, panting. "The hull's integrity is barely holding, though. What the hell is going on?"

Garcia pointed at a nearby aperture. Carbajal pressed his head against the glass. Outside, a massive vortex spun its pinwheel arms, pulling the ship like a gnat down a swirling drain.

"Some kind of wormhole," Garcia said.

"How? This didn't come across our scanners."

"We've been out in space for four generations. *Nothing's* come across our scanners."

Carbajal ran up to the nearest terminal and punched in a slew of commands. "We can ignite the fusion thrusters, propel away at full power."

"I'm doing that now."

"What?"

Garcia grimaced, a look of defeat painting his face. "The pull of that thing's so strong, we can't feel the thrusters do a damn thing."

The eye of the wormhole engulfed the ship like a looming shadow, ominous and awe-inducing all the same. The hull of the ship rattled in protest as metal screeched, the walls beginning to warp. Carbajal pressed his eyes shut as the ship plunged into the heart of darkness.

There'd been a brief moment of silence. Of nothingness. Perhaps that is what death felt like, Carbajal thought. When his eyes opened, he was still inside the *Metzlixochitl*. Everything was still intact. Except the world was quiet. Serene. Like Heaven.

"What the hell happened?" Garcia said, rubbing his head.

Outside the aperture, the ship hovered over an ocean of infinite white. There was almost a sheen to the world, like polished ivory. Carbajal ran toward the opposite side of the bridge. A gaping black hole spun in place.

"What's going on?" Carbajal said.

"Open the main shutters," Garcia said.

Carbajal turned toward the terminal and punched in a few keys. The bridge's main shutters parted, revealing a large panoramic window. Outside, a colossal four-armed being with a long downcurved bill sat hunched over a spindle as it churned out large swaths of white fabric. Its body—which dwarfed the ship many times over— was draped in a flowing white robe, seemingly sewn of the same material.

"Holy crap," Garcia said. "What the hell is that?"

"It looks like an ibis."

"Huh?"

"The bird. Like the Egyptian god Thoth."

The being jerked its head toward the ship. Its eyes were clouded, like milky orbs. "Who goes there?" the thing squawked, its deep voice echoing across the white chasm.

"Quick," Garcia said. "Open the comms. Hit the loudspeaker."

Carbajal flipped a switch and stepped back, nearly tumbling over his chair.

"This is Captain Nolan Garcia," his voice boomed. "I'm alongside my engineer, Ignacio Carbajal. We are stewards of the generation ship *Metzlixochitl*. The MoonFlower. Who are we speaking to?"

The being tilted its head as if gauging the source of the sound. "I am the Tailor. The weaver of the fabric of spacetime. Why are you here?"

"We have been traveling the cosmos looking for a new home."

"A new home?" The Tailor picked up a square patch of fabric and stepped toward the ship, its face contorting in bewilderment.

"We lost our old world to war and plague many years ago," Garcia said, his head stooping. "Our ship holds the last of our kind."

The Tailor nodded. "I know what that is like."

Garcia looked at Carbajal, shrugging.

"I beg your pardon," Garcia said, "but where are we exactly? Our ship fell into some kind of—"

"Wormhole," the Tailor said, nodding. "They tear rampantly across every plane of existence. Some occur when stars collapse on themselves. Sometimes certain beings force them open, thinking they've found a shortcut somewhere. Other times, near their ends, whole worlds are perforated with them until everything is swallowed up. I mend every tear I can. But there are so many, and there is only one of me."

In the distance a black, twirling pit tore open, blemishing the ocean of white.

"That one is from another universe," the Tailor said. "Duty calls. Time to send you back."

The Tailor clutched the ship in one of its hands and gently shoved it back through the hole it came from. With its other hand, it brought down a piece of cloth over the spinning vortex.

Before darkness swallowed the ship whole again, Carbajal noticed a small tear in the Tailor's robe. Within the gash, countless colorful, twinkling spirals swirled inside a sea of ebony. Then, nothing.

———～～～———

They woke in the blackness of space, stars twinkling like gems in the unreachable distance. Garcia eyed Carbajal, pursed his lips, and stared into the vastness with a longing gaze.

For a moment they said nothing, each unsure if what they'd experienced truly happened. How could it? An ancient being mending the tears in the fabric of reality?

Carbajal assumed they'd been suffering space delirium caused by gamma ray bursts. But then again, those would've shown up on the scanners. He slumped in his chair and checked the readouts just to be sure.

"Captain!" Carbajal said. He swiped his fingers frantically over the touchscreen.

"Hm?"

"I'm picking up a new reading. Something that wasn't here before. We're on course for a solar system with a planet that may be hospitable. Not more than..." He checked and double checked. "Forty standard years away."

Garcia hunched over the screen and beamed.

"Well, damn, Carbajal! We may even reach it before we die of old age."

"We'll be heroes. When everyone wakes."

"Very old heroes."

"But boy," Carbajal said. "We'll sure have some stories to tell."

Garcia smiled, the twinkle in his eyes like stars in the dark. "Then let's keep her steady as she goes."

The Protean Tether

He'd dreamt. All his life the dreams had manifested themselves as shapeless terrors come alive in the night. The visions had become frequent and violent over the last few weeks. In this dream, Cypher stood naked on the center of a stone alter. The robed cultists chanted while the gnarled, clawed fingers of the faceless abomination clasped at his torso and ripped the skin from his flesh like a veil. The creature then tore into his abdomen, spilling torrents of black blood and strange viscera.

He always woke before he could scream. On this night he awoke in front of the blinding glare of the terminal's screen. He shielded his face with his hand, waiting for his eyes to adjust.

"Fuck," he said, the back of his head itching in the worst way. He ran his hand along the base of his skull where the tether was still hooked up to his neural shunt. The screen now indicated his mod had completed its download. He quickly killed the terminal and unplugged the tether from the porthole. He approached his window, crimped a single slat from the blinds, and looked out into the street. The light from a neon sign blinked on and off against his face while he scanned for any eavesdroppers. One could never be too sure of who was watching, reporting.

Getting caught tampering with your neural implants was punishable by death. And in the sprawl of Nylax City, if it wasn't the police catching you, there was always an abundance of street rats willing to turn you over for a dime.

Cypher stood from his chair and stretched his arms above his head. The nightmare had made sure he wouldn't be able to sleep again for some time. *Fuck it,* he thought. Might as well test out the new mod with a night on the town.

He stepped out of his apartment building and into the cold night. He lit a cigarette, inhaling its fumes, allowing them to warm his body from the inside. Cypher flicked the cigarette and turned toward the downtown lights.

Making his way around town, Cypher glanced at the protective bubble above the city. It was a clear, starry night, the nebulous spiraled arm of the Milky Way galaxy streaking across the sky. No signs of bombardment like on some occasions. The war had spared this city another night.

On this night, just like any other, the streets were lined with sleeping vagabonds, junkies, and destitute vermin. They reached for a handout, but he had nothing to offer. No money. No drugs. His only drug was the mod itself. It was one of the few ways to get off in this town that didn't kill you outright.

Strolling past the neon signs of the red-light district, the mod booted. A small tingle ran from his head all the way down his spine. He leaned against the wall of a run-down nightclub and let the process kick in.

He gritted his teeth, the colors around him beginning to change. That's how it started.

The standard augmented reality program in everyone's brain presented the world the way people used to see it before the Eldritch invasion two hundred years ago. Apparently, the bastards had unleashed some spore or virus in the air that fucked with everyone's ability to properly grasp reality. Like a permanent bad acid trip. A congenital hallucinogenic nightmare passed from generation to generation.

The mandatory implants kept everyone tethered to the world and free from the madness they'd otherwise experience. Cypher hated it.

If humanity's anchoring to reality was an artificial construct, why not have fun and design a more interesting world? That's why he loved being a bootlegger. It made for a happier populace and kept the money flowing in. And everyone had special requests, too. Some wanted to experience a medieval fantasy world, or a cartoon wonderland. As for him...

He clenched his fists and fell to his knees. The process was always a shock to the mind. A wave of code washed over his vision as buildings digitally reconstructed all around him. He pressed a hand against the wall of the nightclub for support. It transformed from a drab slab of concrete to a shimmering steel wall. He turned around. The snoozing scum on the street became a row of dormant robot-men, slumbering on gold-plated roads embedded with glowing circuits. It was his version of some futuristic utopia.

Cypher steadied himself, taking a few slow steps forward. In days past when he had attempted his first tether crack, he'd experienced a sensory overload, finding himself curled into a ball, crying by the side of a gutter as a mob of alley cats begged him for change.

He looked upward where towers of chrome and glass gleamed in the distance. The city no longer appeared as it truly was; a worn, dying rust hole. It was now as it should've been. As if time had reset, ignoring the near-total annihilation of his species.

It was all an illusion. He knew that. An augmented reality of lies. Outside the dome, the few remnants of humanity still warred with the invading tentacled horrors. But if he was going to live and die in the bubble of Nylax, he'd do it seeing the world he wanted to see.

He strolled into the nightclub, where the thrashing synth beats recomposed themselves into soft orchestral notes. A robotic waitress directed him to the bar. He nodded and forced a smile, nestling himself onto a painful barstool. Perception was one thing; tactile experience was another. *Fuck it.*

A bartending robot hovered over to him and smiled warmly. The illusion was perfect. "What you want, asshole?" Almost perfect.

"Gimme a beer. Strong. And filtered. Not that piss-water you guys make in the back." He slammed a dented coin on the counter and slid it forward.

A horde of robot bodies ground against one another as they danced, many of them entranced under the spell of the week's new designer drug.

The automaton beside him slouched against the bar, staring at his own reflection at the bottom of the mug. He rubbed his shiny chin and shook his head. "It's a nightmare out there, ain't it?"

"I don't follow," Cypher said.

"I take it you've never seen one?"

Cypher knew what the guy was talking about. He wasn't, however, sure he wanted to have this conversation. "Should I have?"

The robot shook his head. "It'll drive you to madness. Caught a glimpse of one once. Name's Jules, by the way." He took a sip.

"I'm Cypher."

"Cypher?"

"Well, between me and you, Jules, that's my street name. My name's Kal Thulus."

"Nice to meet you, Kal."

"Likewise, Jules. So, tell me about the monsters."

Jules dragged in a deep breath. "I used to work in the sewers. The city drains flow and empty outside the bubble. Few years back there was a big blockage, so me and a few guys got sent out to clear it. We were outside Nylax, out in the wasteland, when our tethers' signals started to fade. My vision got weird, man. And then I fucking saw...something."

"Something?"

"It was, I don't know, a mass. A jumble of squirmy, slimy, I don't know what."

The bartender tilted Cypher's glass and poured the beer, shooting the drunkard an ugly stare.

"What happened next?"

Jules leaned in and said, "The thing freakin' reached out to me. I screamed. We all screamed. Then we jolted back to the city. And you know what happened next? The cops. They had us all lobotomized." He turned to face Cypher. "Can't you see the scar? Can't you see it?" He pointed to a rusted scrape across his metallic head.

Cypher turned away.

As the bartender served him his beer, a police officer stepped through the door. Cypher had programmed the mod so that cops would be left unaltered in case he found himself in a pinch. The cop wore a full getup of plated black tactical armor and slung a shiny machine gun around his shoulder. He was turning his head every which way, looking for something specific. Cypher knew the look; he was on the prowl.

Cypher knocked back a sip of bitter beer and swiveled away from the cop. He decided he'd rather not be seen. Only thing worse than a murderer in Nylax City was a bootlegger. As he took another sip, he felt the sweat drip down the side of his head. No way the cops were onto him. He'd been careful; his every client had been carefully vetted; every program had been wiped after every transaction.

"Hey," the cop called out while Cypher raised his glass again.

Cypher looked at his mug; the cop's reflection became gradually larger until a powerful hand clutched his shoulder and spun him around.

The cop leaned his head into his chest and spoke into his comm. "Yeah, I got him."

"What the fuck is this about?" Cypher said.

The cop looked down on Cypher with a sinister scowl. "You're under arrest for the illicit manufacturing of unauthorized tether modifications."

"Fuck off."

The cop grabbed Cypher's arm, pivoted, and threw him over his shoulder. Cypher landed on the floor, slamming the back of his head like a melon. Moisture seeped from his skull and pooled on the ground. Cypher's eyes settled on the cop, who was now slinging his rifle around.

Suddenly Jules speared his shoulder into the cop's body, tackling him to the floor.

"Run, stupid!" Jules shouted.

Cypher pushed off the floor and slipped on the pool of blood, striking his head on the floor again. "Fuck!" he cried out. A sharp pain pulsed through his temples. He shook the thought and darted for the door.

As he sprinted out the nightclub, he heard the thunder of the rifle's shot at his back.

While he ran, he skimmed a hand across the back of his head. His porthole was cracked and leaking blood. It was hot and thick like used synthetic oil.

The world around him suddenly glitched, sharp lines cracking across his field of view. The faces of onlookers distorted into odd shapes, the peculiarity of their geometry frightening to behold. Their mouths had morphed into abysmal, sharp-toothed maws, and their faces became forms of melted flesh baring multiple sets of eyes, all watching him run fervently across the cracked streets.

Above his head, purple arcs of lightning streaked across the night sky. Beyond the lightning, a torrent of shooting stars pierced the atmosphere like molten rain.

Cypher slipped past the throngs downtown and found himself in the industrial section of Nylax, where the machines churned and smoke spiraled upward, staining the ceiling of the dome.

He stopped and peered behind his shoulder. The cop was in pursuit, only a few meters behind him now. His pursuer took a knee and raised his rifle.

Cypher spotted a large storm drain directly beneath the shadow of an abandoned factory and dove in. The currents of the sewer's rapids whisked him down a labyrinthine series of leaden pipes. The putrid smell of waste and death crawled into his nostrils, stinging his eyes.

He twisted past one last juncture and spotted what appeared to be the end of the tunnel. At its end he caught a glimpse of small, twinkling lights. Sliding down, they speckled and glimmered madly, as if inviting him into the grasp of their illumination.

He neared the mouth of the tunnel and realized he'd been looking at stars. Clear, unfiltered stars.

The water pressure spat him out of the drain and down into the bottom of a small ravine. He tumbled down a rocky, shrub-ridden hill, scraping his limbs until his body settled flat on its back at the bottom of a marsh.

The downpour of meteorites continued their assault on the air, while strange nebulous clouds spewed flashes of purple light. On the horizon, twin scarlet moons watched over the sky like silent sentries.

Cypher pushed off the mud and tumbled forward into a swath of tall, thin weeds. He speared both hands into the brush to part the grass when the glitching started again. Then the skin of his hands began to peel and flake like the embers of a dying drum fire.

Underneath the veneer of soft, pink skin lay green, scaled flesh. His fingers were now long and writhing, his nails hooked and sharp.

"What? No, no, no! What the fuck is going on?" Cypher screamed, holding both hands in front of his face.

Suddenly the muscles on his back began to twitch uncontrollably, his flesh writhing and spasming like a bubbling soup. His spine birthed two long erect bones that then began to bend like the legs of a spider.

He reached a hand to his back. Attached to their frames were the leathery trappings of what felt like batwings.

A thunderclap rocked the heavens. A large fireball lit the earth, blinding him for a few moments before the night returned to reclaim its domain. A small squadron of sleek, angular fighters zipped across the sky like angry hornets.

In the sky, a giant one-eyed mass of black-fleshed tentacles swarmed and flailed about, lashing at the jet fighters buzzing around it. The creature moaned when they fired upon it, their projectiles piercing its flesh.

What was happening?

Cypher slogged through the marsh, clawing through the thick brush. He climbed out of the ravine and his exhausted body collapsed on the ground, his lungs burning while they gasped for breath.

Before the world turned black, a pair of robed men stood above him, ogling his monstrous visage.

"Call the others," one of them said. "We've got another one."

Then Cypher closed his eyes and embraced the ensuing darkness.

⌁

He awoke inside a cave, lying on a flat slab of cold stone. It was dark and humid, and the air had a moist, fungal scent to it. The world was tactile and full of smells and sounds no dream could ever replicate. Not even the most lucid.

The robed men returned, along with a few women, their faces obscured by their pointed hoods. A dozen of them, all in line, humming in a low pitch. Their chants reverberated across the stone walls and the hollow earth. They then circled him with their heads bowed, like mourners at a funeral procession. Then and there, they'd appeared like crazed zealots. Cultists. Like the ones in his dreams.

And as he looked about, the terrors approached from the depths of the caverns like living, crawling shadows.

Twenty of them, maybe more.

Some of the aberrations appeared as squirming, gelatinous masses with countless rows of unblinking eyes. They trundled forward, leaving behind a trail of slimy discharge.

Others appeared as impossible anomalies; serpents with wings, or toad-like humanoids with webbed hands and feet.

Cypher tried to stand but couldn't. It was as if some powerful force kept him pulled against the rock. One of the cultists approached him and gently soothed his head. "We've removed the tether. All will be revealed. Not all of us agreed with what happened. Don't forget those who tried to help you."

The cultist stepped aside, bowed, and swept a hand toward Cypher. The terrors encircled him. He groaned and writhed on the slab, trying desperately to scream, but no sound would form.

A chorus of voices penetrated his head, all speaking in tongues until they unified into a single, guttural tone.

Cypher. Kal Thulus. You have slept the sleep of ages and have dreamed a dream of a thousand years. Now you have begun to wake.

"Where am I? Who are you?" Cypher forced the words from his mouth. As he spoke a sliver of ooze trickled down his lips and off his chin like spilled porridge.

You are safe inside the earth. Away from the invaders. We are of a kind.

"No," he said, pushing out the word with his tongue, spilling even more fluid down his face. "You are the invaders."

We are home. This is our home. You are home.

"My home is in Nylax City. You killed us all. My people." The ooze became thicker, now bubbling in his mouth.

We speak the language of dreams. For eons our words traveled the cosmos. The Men-Kin received the words and called them nightmares. Then Men-Kin traveled the stars and discovered our home and slew our kind and called us terrible things. We returned their gesture of war. Our captured kin had their minds imprisoned in the false reality of the bubble. You became a prisoner, and we mourned. The tether tricks the mind. You are free now, Kal Thulus. Kal Thulu. KalThulu. Ka'Thulu. K'Thulhu.

"N-no," he gurgled, the salty liquid freely seeping from his mouth. The fluid smelled of brine. Salt water. He tilted his head and looked down at his chest. A squirming mass of tentacles erupted from his mouth, spewing bitter slime while his teeth chattered with anger.

This couldn't be real. But the words in his head. They felt warm, loving, a truth beyond the reach of lies and illusions. And the dreams all those years; the echoes of brethren calling to him.

He sat upright and swung his arms in the air. They were supple and powerful, like the trunks of elder trees. The wings at his back sprouted outward and caught a draft of warm wind like an ancient sail. He threw his legs over the slab and vaulted onto the floor. The ground quaked with his fury as the memories returned.

The Men-Kin. The invaders. Set foot on ancient soil. Brought fire and ruin as gifts and called his brethren devils. He stumbled out of the cave as the rest of them watched from the shadows.

The wasteland greeted him, where once rolled lush hills dense with golden poppies, and where the milkweeds swayed to the warm summer currents. What had become of his beautiful home?

He'd remembered then: who he was, what this all had been. His bones moaned as his muscles strained and stretched, and before he'd realized, he had grown larger than the spires in Nylax City.

K'Thulhu marched toward the dome, the bubble of rot and decay, of shackles and lost dreams. The Men-Kin jet fighters swarmed beside his face, pricking him with their beams and rockets, but he ignored them like the gnats they were. He lifted his arms to the sky like an offering to even older gods and brought down his fists with the fury of a thousand years.

The glass cracked and fissured and burst into a million pieces.

And he looked inside and beheld the peculiar, beautiful shapes of his brethren.

And he smiled, for soon they would once again share their dreams together.

The Carnivorous Planet

The gears clanked as they labored to hoist Alpha Base's eastern gate open. A wave of afternoon heat swept through the colony, sparing no person bustling down its busy streets. Despite the sweat trickling down her torso, a shiver ran down Sergeant Kiyana Katan's body, turning the hairs on her skin prickly inside her combat armor. She shouldered her rucksack, cocked her assault rifle, and inhaled a breath of cool, filtered air through her facemask.

As the gate opened, a pair of bulldozers rolled slowly in, splatters of blood painting the sides of their colossal tracks. She offered the drivers a nod before looking upon the verdant, monolithic wonder of the planet's biosphere just waiting to swallow her whole. Everywhere her eyes settled lay jungle so thick and gnarled sunlight seldom penetrated its canopy.

And in that darkness the terrors awaited.

Katan gritted her teeth, turned away, and fought the urge to vomit. *Don't let the fear consume you. You've got a job to do.* She turned, forcing herself to look at the swath of trees past the clearing. She remembered when she'd first set foot on the planet and gazed upon the lush vegetation, the majestic mountains, the steep waterfalls, her first sunset. The wonder and awe of it all had almost been too much for her to process. Now, it was different. Now, she longed to leave.

A pair of colonists heaving broken turret components into a loader eyed her with what she perceived to be pity. They knew she was being fed to the wolves. It seemed everyone on Alpha Base had heard the rumors of the nightmares lurking in the shadows of their new home. *Scions,* they'd been called. Not many things frightened her in this life, but what she'd heard about those monstrosities made her want to believe in God.

Her facemask blipped as the mission dossier streamed in from Command and a list of pictures toggled through her HUD. Five soldiers and a scientist. All had failed to report back to Alpha Base the previous night from a geological survey just a few kilometers northeast of their location.

She'd known Command had struggled with the option of a rescue operation against further potential losses. In the months before, grunts like her had been disposable resources to them but the scientist, ultimately, sold them on the mission go-ahead. His knowledge of the planet was deemed too valuable for the colony's chances of success.

The poor bastard—a senior geologist named Herzog—had the honor of naming the planet *Jannah*, the old Arabic word for 'garden.' The same Garden of Paradise from Earth's old theological texts. Cruelly, they had learned Jannah was no paradise. But with the remnants of humanity facing extinction, it had been too little too late to turn away from the first habitable world to be discovered in centuries since the Exodus. Besides, there was nowhere else to turn except back toward the cold vastness of space.

A dropship and a pair of bombers roared overhead and settled into a slow hover until they touched down on Alpha's southern landing port. They were the latest gifts trickling in from the generation ship *DawnStar*. At the rate they'd been receiving reinforcements from the generation ship, the planet would surely reclaim what belonged to it in no time.

At her back, the new recruits inspected their gear before sendoff. Privates Vlasov, Raynes, and Merchant huddled together, gossiping as a means to dispel the terror boring through their spines. They'd never ventured past the gates. Few had. She'd only hazarded a handful of trips herself on some tedious brush clearance duties on the edge of base.

"Can you guys believe Katan's leading this?" Vlasov whispered, cradling his assault rifle nervously against his chest.

"Why'd they even toss a fem into the Army?" Raynes said as he adjusted the flashlight on his shoulder with a trembling hand. "We need them up on the *DawnStar* for breeding."

Merchant shook his head and spat out a wad of tobacco before securing the facemask over his head. "Naw, man, she's infertile. You can't pick up a baby, you get to pick up a rifle. Rules. You fuckers gotta learn to read the combat manual."

Before Katan could rein them in, Mia Halvorsen jogged toward the gate. She had been outfitted in a full reconnaissance suit like the rest of them: standard ballistic helmet, electronic face mask with oxygen filter, camouflaged combat armor, waterproof boots, heavy duty fatigues. Halvorsen, lean and wiry, stood a good six inches taller than Katan herself, and her face carried the well-preserved appearance of someone who'd been spared heavy labor aboard the *DawnStar*. Katan had seen her frequenting the colony's tavern, slogging back the piss-water they called beer while waving off the shouts of drunken suitors. Halvorsen's dossier streamed down Katan's facemask as she approached. Thirty-two, biologist, single, no family aboard the *DawnStar*.

"Sergeant Katan," Halvorsen said, "I've been assigned by Colonel Assad to accompany you."

"On what grounds?" Katan asked, dismissing the dossier from view with a blink.

"I'm a biologist. I worked closely with Mattias Herzog collecting samples out there."

"Sorry. Doesn't qualify you for a search and rescue party."

"With all due respect, Sergeant, I've ventured into that jungle. You haven't. I think that qualifies me enough."

The squad looked on. She saw the contempt beaming in their eyes; their lives were in her hands, and they detested every second they were under her command.

She considered reprimanding Halvorsen.

Save your battles for hills worth dying on, her father's voice rang in her head. It was an old adage, he had told her, from a world whose hills he'd never seen, and which had long burned away. She wondered if it held merit these days on this world and on these hills. She bit her lip. "Stay close and don't get in the way. Anything we need to know, you call it out. The colony can't afford more losses." She turned to face the men. Not a single man was older than twenty years. She felt pity for them. Neither the boot camp nor the simulations aboard the *DawnStar* could have possibly prepared them for real world survival. How could it? No single human had seen military combat in hundreds of years.

Katan turned toward the wilderness. "Remember," she said. "Once we cross into the jungle, our radio's gonna be useless unless we can get to clear ground. We stay keen and watch each other's backs and we'll be in and out before dusk. Alright, we all know our orders. Let's move."

The gate clamped down as they departed Alpha Base, sealing the five of them off from the colony. At their backs, the base stood lonesome on the edge of the valley with the majestic Shinjo Mountains at its back where Command had anchored the quarry. The base was a small foothold—one she expected to grow exponentially in the months and years to come. In the meantime, those who'd been sent to Jannah had a duty to secure Alpha and clear more tracts of land for future expansion projects. This was a crash course in survival for every person involved as humanity nudged itself into a world fighting to keep it out.

Often, when she'd lie awake at night, she wondered how the other generation ships that had fanned out ages ago had fared. If they'd been successful in finding habitable worlds. She supposed she'd never know.

Fifty paces out and the ground underneath their heels crunched as their boots trotted over glass: the remnants of the orbital strike that cleared the five-mile swath of land for the construction of Alpha Base. Beyond the glass, patches of white grass had begun to spring resiliently from the ground where they'd once been singed. Sensing the squad's approaching vibrations, the vines on the edge of the jungle squirmed and retracted into small mounds inside the earth.

Private Merchant, running point, nervously stepped over a grass crab as it scuttled past him and dove into a patch of tall, cilia-like pasture. The blades of translucent grass swayed at the mercy of a warm breeze while the crab dug its mandibles into the soil.

"Fuck," he yelled, swinging his rifle around.

"Hold your fire," Katan said. "We're running white phosphorus rounds on this mission. We don't want a fire spreading too close to base. Besides, those things are only scavengers."

"Yes, ma'am." Merchant nervously watched the creature burrow into the dirt before turning to continue his march.

"Phosphorus rounds?" Halvorsen asked.

"That's right," Katan said. "The tips shatter on impact, releasing small amounts of white phosphorus. Once it comes into contact with oxygen, it sets off a small combustion. Hard to extinguish."

"Isn't that overkill? Those kinds of weapons were long barred from combat use on Earth."

"Earth?" Katan scoffed. "You know what we're dealing with out here. Fire's our best chance. Bullets don't always pierce every target, but everything burns."

The biologist regarded the tree line on the horizon and nodded. "Curious," Halvorsen said, now pulling up beside Katan. "How'd Command make you a sergeant? We haven't engaged in military operations in generations. Not sure how the chain of command works these days."

"I was security on the *DawnStar*. Worked my way up from corrections to armed detail. Went from corralling junkies and killers in the slammer to guarding cryo chambers, crowd control, you name it." Katan exhaled a deep breath. "I'm also sterile, so... I guess they liked me enough to fit me with a rifle and slap a sergeant's patch on my shoulder. Can't raise a family so I get to lead soldiers. With all these questions I take it you're a Sleeper?"

Halvorsen nodded and smiled. "You got me. You'll have to forgive me. I've been under cryo since we set out from Earth, waiting until the council decided they needed my expertise. Now I've been thawed out, I'm not too aware of daily life routines that have evolved aboard the *DawnStar*. Sorry for asking, but how exactly are you sterile? I know there are geneticists on the ship. Surely that's something they could have corrected."

"You must have been thawed out just this week. Two hundred years after the Exodus there was a population boom no one was prepared for. There were only so many resources aboard that ship and we could only grow so much food and feed so many mouths. The situation led to a civil war for control over those resources. After that debacle, the council decided to draw a lottery from that point forward. Children were selected at random for sterilization procedures in an effort to reign in the population crisis. I drew that end of the stick and here I am on this big killer petri dish of a planet."

"I don't envy you, Sergeant," she whispered. "You went from dealing with the worst of the worst up there to having to deal with whatever haunts these jungles, all while I slept cozy in a cryo pod. You're an asset to the human race."

Katan thought of the scions. Knots twisted in her stomach. At least it felt that way. She'd been briefed on their existence shortly before the mission, but she'd refused to believe it could be true. How could it? She supposed a lifetime aboard a cold, floating raft couldn't prepare the mind for anything so horrible.

Katan looked to the sky one last time before entering the jungle. The generation ship *DawnStar* hung in orbit like a small moon, framed against a beautiful blue-green backdrop. The starving, overpopulated remnants of humankind waited while she and the rest did their best to secure a new home. She knew she'd never set foot up there again and, one way or another, she would die on Jannah.

"Why couldn't they send more people down here, Sergeant?" Vlasov asked, noticing her gaze. "We're getting buried on the daily. I mean, there's like three million people up there, right? And they sent, what, three thousand down here?"

"Just for now," Halvorsen interjected. "We're not aware of all the dangers on Jannah. All it takes is one big viral outbreak and there goes humankind."

"Well, at least we know the air is breathable," Raynes said. "And the food and resources here are abundant. That's a start, right?"

Halvorsen nodded. "True, except for the venomous fauna, toxic flora, and countless strains of spores in the air. That's why we wear facemasks. This world has a rich biodiversity like Earth's. Much of it dangerous to us."

"Yup," Merchant said, clearing a path through a pair of large ferns, "we learned what some of the microbial life can do to us already. I mean, we all saw what happened to Ortega's insides, all turned inside out and crawling with worms."

"That's enough," Katan said. "From here on out keep communications to a minimum. If I'm not mistaken some of the plant life on this world is very acute to sound vibrations."

"That's right, Sergeant," Halvorsen said. "Numerous plants and animals on this planet rely on countless defense mechanisms, many of which we're still learning about."

"Is it true what they say about the scions?" Vlasov asked, a tremor in his voice. "I heard they're demons and this planet is a bridge between our world and Hell. A guy I know who works night watch told me he saw one staggering on the far edge of base last week."

The men stopped and waited for an answer. Halvorsen turned away from their gazes, beads of sweat dotting her forehead.

"That's classified," Katan butted in. "Just shut up and stay sharp. Anything approaches you in an unfriendly manner, you light it up."

As they crossed into the jungle, only scattered slivers of sunlight pierced the dense vegetation, most of it shimmering on wet ferns or glistening like diamonds across the eyes of winged insects. Five minutes in and the squad could seldom see the world beneath their knees as they slogged through muddied earth, pulling themselves forward on the nooks in between the bark of large trees.

Things creaked and croaked around them, as did the sounds of leaves rustling in the canopy above their heads. Katan ordered the squad to activate their shoulder mounted flashlights and keep vigilant.

As their lights cut across the darkness, the rich biosphere became apparent; everywhere around them thrived diverse species of trees, insects, and luminescent fungi. In those confines, the air grew humid and heavy, and Katan felt her fatigues wrap tightly around her body as her skin became damp with sweat. Despite the filters in her mask, the waft of rot crept into her nostrils, the heat carrying the unwanted scents of death and decay on its currents.

On the banks of a small marsh, she stepped over a webwork of thin, taut vines. Tiny dead insects hung on them like bait. She knew if nature was remotely intelligent, those were the trappings of some carnivorous plant lurking in a dark trench nearby. She motioned the squad to tread cautiously.

Katan scanned the jungle for traces of the expedition but found no tracks, expended casings, or bloodied soil. Nothing. If the traces had been there, the ecosystem had surely swallowed them in the short time since the party had gone missing.

The deeper their descent into the jungle, the louder the air around them buzzed. Not like the electric drone of computers or the air cycling systems aboard the *DawnStar*, but the mad cacophony of insects, the rustling of palms, and the screeching of unseen things stalking them in the distance. The world bombarded her senses. She wasn't used to seeing and hearing so much at once. All life on the ship could be reduced to the quiet, monotonous routines of eating, sleeping, and laborious maintenance work.

She shook the thought and forced her mind to focus on the jungle floor. Her HUD overlaid a digital path as it calculated the survey team's projected path. The route had led them over a mile from the outskirts of the colony.

"We're beyond the one-mile safety line," Katan said. "Their plotted course lists their mission two miles northeast of Alpha. That's too far out from base for them to have any proper security detail. This doesn't make sense. What was Herzog working on that was so important he couldn't stay within secure parameters?"

Halvorsen stopped to lean against the broad trunk of a tree. "I can't discuss the particulars, but I can say we discovered a lifeform that may affect our safety as a species. An entire ecosystem, to be exact. It's important we locate him and gather what information he may have uncovered."

"Holy fuck," Merchant said. "Why the hell weren't we told? Call me crazy, but that sounds a little too dangerous for just the five of us to tackle."

"That does sound sketchy, Sergeant," Vlasov said, turning to Katan. "I mean, if it's a threat to our whole fucking species, I'm not sure I'm qualified to handle that. Why don't they send a dropship to survey the area?"

"Take a look, Private," Katan said, tilting her head toward the canopy. The trees, vines, and leaves had interlocked so tightly they had formed a near complete barrier from the sky.

Vlasov scowled. "Yeah? Then why not send fifty guys out here with us?"

"Command won't spare too many soldiers outside the gates at any given time. Alpha needs every able-bodied person to defend the colony."

"You're telling us whatever's out there poses that great a threat?" Merchant said.

Halvorsen looked down at her boots.

The men eyed her like a pack of angry dogs. Katan stepped between the biologist and her men.

"So what, exactly," Raynes said, "are we fucking walking into?"

A shriek cut across the air. A grouping of small ferns rustled ten yards northeast of their location. Merchant spun and dropped to a knee, raising his rifle. Katan waved Halvorsen behind her as she lifted her weapon.

Raynes and Vlasov scurried up behind Merchant and covered his left and right flanks.

A young man in tattered military fatigues emerged from the darkness of the brush and into the beams of the squad's lights. Heavy perforations dotted his combat armor, while ribbons of flailed skin dangled over his body. A vertical gash ran across his belly, leaving his intestines to drag behind him as he ambled forward.

The man's lips quivered as he attempted to form words. "Who. Speaks. For. The. Flesh."

"Holy fuck," Merchant said lowering his rifle. "Sergeant?"

Katan's HUD scanned the soldier's face. Private Chase Fulton, eighteen years old. Missing as of last night.

"Private Fulton," she called out, "I'm Sergeant Kiyana Katan. Stay right where you are. We'll come administer medical attention, son." She knelt down and hurriedly unshouldered her rucksack. Her medkit wasn't suited to treat life-threatening injuries, but perhaps she could try to minimize some of the pain until they hauled the poor kid back to base.

"Halvorsen," Katan said as she rummaged through her pack. "What in the hell did that to him?"

Halvorsen watched Fulton, her eyes trained on him as he stepped clearly into view. "I'm not sure, but we'll know soon enough."

Katan trotted toward Fulton, her medkit in tow. Fulton lumbered forward, his skin pallid, blue. As he approached the squad, Katan noticed movement inside the gape in his torso. She adjusted her shoulder lamp and focused her light on the wound. A tangled mass of green, writhing fibers stirred amongst globs of what appeared to be coagulated blood. "Halvorsen?"

"Fuck," Halvorsen shouted. "Scion!"

Green tendrils shot from Fulton's belly, slashing madly at the air around him. A few strands slithered inquisitively up a pair of branches, moving like feelers.

"Light him up!" Katan yelled. She crouched, slung her rifle upward, and took aim.

Before anyone could fire a round, a tendril shot out from Fulton's belly and wrapped itself around Merchant's neck. Fine, spindly barbs blossomed from the tendril, plunging themselves into his flesh like serrated teeth. Merchant tossed his head back and let loose a gurgled scream that fogged up his facemask.

Katan lined her sights on Fulton's head, but Merchant staggered into the path of the writhing mass. In an instant, the tendril reeled back inside Fulton's stomach, sawing through Merchant's throat as it retracted. Merchant's head fell by the wayside, a few strands of tissue still connecting his head to his neck. He took one wobbly step forward before his body toppled into the mud, the impact finally severing his head.

Fulton sprinted forward, stalks of green shoots bursting from his eyeballs. He screeched. His mouth stretched so far the skin on his face ripped apart, until his lower mandible dislodged itself completely and splashed into a muddy puddle.

Vlasov and Raynes opened fire, their rounds piercing Fulton's torso, shredding his insides. Some rounds exited out his back and slammed into the trees behind him. A few rounds struck his combat jacket, igniting on impact.

It took a few moments before Fulton became engulfed in flames, his limbs flailing in pain. Pain, Katan thought, was a universal language, shared amongst men and monsters alike.

Katan raised her rifle. Fulton turned so that he was facing her directly, his tongue hanging limply out the gape in his mouth. She opened fire. His head exploded like a pumpkin, spewing blood, slime, and what appeared to be seed pods into the air.

Fulton dropped, moaning as the fire consumed his body and shriveled his skin. Then, only the sound of crackling flames filled the jungle.

"What the fuck was that?" Raynes screamed.

Halvorsen cautiously approached Merchant's body before turning to examine Fulton's burning corpse, now giving off thick plumes of smoke. "That was a scion."

"And what exactly," Vlasov said through gritted teeth, "*is* a scion?"

Halvorsen crossed her arms over her chest. "I'm not at liberty—"

Katan jabbed a finger in Halvorsen's direction. "Halvorsen, I think it's fucking time you told these men what they're fighting."

The biologist watched as the flames finally consumed what remained of Fulton. Flakes of skin and plant matter peeled off his body, sweeping away into currents of hot air like dry leaves. "We discovered peculiar swaths of land we named hatcheries, scattered across the jungle, wherein a particular breed of carnivorous plant grows. The plant itself is a sort of pod which lies on the ground like an open flower. This pod snaps shut on any creature unlucky enough to get caught in its snare, gestating it by breaking it down into a liquefied substance. We're not sure of the exact process, but it then absorbs its prey's DNA and creates clones, or bastardized hybrids, comprised of plant matter and flesh. We named them scions. What happened to Fulton, though, I've never seen that. It looked like he may have broken loose from the gestation process. Maybe he was under some kind of mind control." She threw her arms in the air. "I don't fucking know."

"We've lost dozens of men in these jungles in the last few months. Have you seen these cloned scions?"

She bit her lip. "Only their remains."

"Why are we dying out here? Why are these plants so important?" Katan asked.

"We collected samples from various cloned animals and even studied their behavior from afar, observing their roaming habits, their lifespans, their aggression toward other lifeforms. The scions carry seedlings inside them, traverse where the pods couldn't physically venture, integrate into their respective kingdoms, and propagate the seeds across the planet."

"Planet?" Raynes said. "You mean those things grow everywhere on Jannah?"

"We think they do."

The men groaned.

"So what did Herzog set out here to do?" Katan asked.

"We're not too far out from a local hatchery. Last week Herzog began excavating the site and discovered an intricate web of connective dendrites linking hatcheries to each other. We believe they impart information amongst themselves, like the vibrations of nearby animals, dangers to the area like approaching wildfires; all like a network sharing data with itself."

"What do you mean?" Katan said. "You're saying these plants can communicate with each other? Across all of Jannah?"

"That's what we think. The planet appears to be connected by these underground networks of sensory, data-sharing roots. Like a giant nervous system or neural network. Command flew a few survey drones over Herzog's site. Laser mapping detected odd contours in the ground hidden by dense swaths of foliage. The further we mapped the area, the more we observed peculiar geometric depressions underneath the land. Yesterday, Herzog was to return to continue his operations."

"Fuck it all," Katan said. "Any more bad news?"

"In regards to the pods, we also observed that once a sample of an organism's DNA is integrated into their collective databanks, that particular animal can be cloned in perpetuity by any of the hatcheries."

"Meaning, in theory, those things can create an endless army of zombified humans and animal hybrids and tear us apart."

"In theory. We don't know if they're self-aware, or how they respond to large scale threats, or hell, if they even see us as a threat at this point. We just don't know. Herzog wanted to continue excavating to see just how extensive these underground dendrites really are, and if they play a part in the anomalies in the earth. We were going to run a series of tests to see exactly what we're dealing with. It may be that all plant life on this world relays some kind of information back on itself. If it does, we may have declared war on the entire ecosystem the minute we bombed Jannah and erected Alpha Base."

"So," Raynes said, "we're sitting on one big ass death trap."

"No fucking way!" Vlasov yelled. "This can't be happening." He took a step backward, tripped over a root, and landed on the side of his face, shattering his facemask. A blast of pressurized air erupted from the cracks. He fumbled with his mask before vomiting into it.

Katan crouched beside him and wrenched the mask from his face. "Get up, Private," she said, hauling him up by the scruff of his combat jacket.

"Wait," Halvorsen said, "there might be spores in the air."

"He can't fight if he can't see. If he gets sick, we'll deal with it as it comes. Raynes, Vlasov, get ready to move out." She tossed the rucksack around her back and inspected her magazine.

"What?" Raynes said. "Sergeant, we can't go on. That scientist is dead. Those soldiers are dead. And if we go, we'll be dead, too. It may not mean much to you, but I got a wife and a baby on the *DawnStar*, for mercy's sake. I actually got something to live for."

Katan swallowed a dry lump. The words stung. She knew she'd never breed or start a family. Long after her tears had dried during those early phases of her adult life, she'd even told herself it didn't matter. Finding a home had always been the goal. For every person on that ship. That's what mattered. Every person on the *DawnStar* and in that colony was now a member of her family. She couldn't let them down.

"We don't know that anyone besides Fulton is dead," Katan said, kneeling besides Merchant's corpse. She retrieved his rifle and plucked three magazines from his combat jacket. "We've already come this far. It's also likely those things know we're here and are heading for us now. If we can find the rest of the men, we'll have a better chance to make it out of here alive so you can all see your families again. Besides, whatever intel Herzog may have gathered could be crucial for the survival of our species. We can't turn back now, we're in it for good." Katan approached Halvorsen and handed her Merchant's rifle. "And that means every one of us is going to do their part."

"But I—"

"Every person on this planet fights, regardless of their role."

Halvorsen nodded as she dug the rifle's butt between her armpit and shoulder.

Vlasov straightened out and wiped the vomit off his face with the cuff of his sleeve. "Roger that, Sergeant."

Raynes stared at Merchant lying in a pool of bloodied mud before falling in with the rest of the squad.

<hr>

They traversed a few tracts of callous jungle, crossing thick swaths of mud and brooks whose banks were infested with malicious spiders. The pointed thistles of flowers cut into their fatigues, a few embedding themselves into their limbs, cursing their skin with flaring rashes.

Halvorsen tried to dispel some of the dread with conversation. She went on about how some wars on Earth were fought in settings not unlike Jannah. Vietnam was a country, she mentioned, whose ecology proved to be the deciding factor in its soldiers staving off the monolithic might of an imperialist enemy. The sprawl of endless jungle offered too much cover for any effective aerial bombardment. Only a long, drawn-out war of attrition could be waged, a conflict where troops fought on equal terms; a strategy that proved too costly for the imperialist powers. Though Katan knew she wasn't to be as blessed, the Earthers had the luxury of calling it quits and returning home. To date, no one on Jannah had that option.

After an hour they came upon the edge of a ravine. From her vantage point, Katan could see a ring of flat, verdant land populated by thick open petals waiting to snap shut like bear traps. Rows of long thorns lined the inner casings of their membranes, ensuring their prey would end up impaled and immobilized. Swaths of tall, thin trees encircled the hatchery, providing ample cover from any serious aerial maneuvers.

Beneath the ravine, she spotted a small trench dug directly into the earth. Various mining tools littered the vicinity of the excavation site, but she saw no traces of human activity. Not even corpses.

"Try to radio Herzog," Katan ordered Vlasov. "See if we can get some short-range frequencies working."

Vlasov nodded, approached the edge of the precipice, and touched his index finger to the side of his helmet. "Doctor Mattias Herzog, this is Private Andrej Vlasov, do you copy?" He flicked the small antenna protruding from his head. "Doctor Herzog, do you copy? Anybody?" There came only the sound of soft crackling.

Katan looked upon the hatchery and noticed a few of the pods were already shut and sealed, their bodies resembling the shapes of peapods. Before she could ask, Halvorsen said, "Hate to alarm you, Sergeant, but we should get moving. Those pods are either digesting something or creating scions as we speak. Either way, I don't recommend we stay long."

She turned to Vlasov. "Anything?"

"Nothing," he said. "This is the place where radio signals come to die."

"Okay," Katan sighed. "Let's get a quick look down there."

They descended the ravine, where a narrow stream of water trickled and collected into a pond below. A scattering of vibrant lilies drifted lazily on the surface of the water. Katan managed a smile. Beauty, she thought, could exist in even the most horrid of places.

As they trekked across the pond, the sediment under their boots shifted. Suddenly the lilies began vibrating and thrashing their petals, causing them to splash on the surface of the water like an alarm.

"What's going on?" Katan asked Halvorsen.

Before she could answer, a dozen pods shifted twenty yards away. Then, their petals blossomed open, revealing their creations. The nude bodies of twelve humanoid males emerged from their cocoons, covered in a green, mucus-like substance. Scions.

As they staggered forward, she caught a better look. They could almost pass for human if it weren't for the subtle green tint of their skin, the black of their gums, and the long, pointed tips of their nails. Their tongues writhed wildly out of their mouths, like a serpent sensing the air around it. It took all of two seconds for them to catch their prey's scent. The scions spun towards the squad and shrieked.

Katan's HUD pinged as it recognized the faces of former colonists, long logged as dead in Command's databanks. Her gut wrenched.

Just then a grouping of thin oblong tendrils sprang out of the water. Small hooked spines protracted from their tips, slashing at the air around them. One tendril reeled into a coil and snapped at Katan's face mask, cracking the glass and knocking her back into the water. All she could see was the torrent of foaming bubbles and the web of broken glass. Her heart knocked against her chest as the adrenaline kicked in.

Vlasov reached a hand out to her. Before she could grasp it, a pair of tendrils dug their hooks into his eyes and pulled him down toward the bottom of the pond. Blood spewed upward, tinting the water red as the rest of the tendrils pummeled him in unison, pinning his body against the sediment below. The water bubbled violently where Vlasov thrashed and kicked for a moment before stopping completely.

Raynes pulled Katan up by her collar and dragged her to the banks of the pond, where Halvorsen was already aiming down her sights. Katan followed Halvorsen's gaze. The scions charged across the field, their bodies now engulfed in flailing, squirming tangles of barbed vines.

She removed her facemask and scowled, a trickle of blood seeping from her mouth. "Gun those fuckers down!" She swung her rifle up to eye level, propped it firmly against her armpit, and fired off a series of three-round bursts. Her first target took a volley of lead to the chest, knocking it back three feet. Before the scion could push itself up, its body had combusted in a flash of blue flames. She scanned a new target, pulled the trigger three times, and watched its head burst.

Raynes wasted little time and immediately dropped to a knee, took aim, and fired. He dropped two scions in two shots, his rounds blowing out their eyeballs, causing their heads to catch fire.

Halvorsen lifted her rifle and let out a burst of automatic fire. The kick from the recoil sent a torrent of lead spraying into a wall of flesh and grass. In moments, flames erupted from the clearing, spreading along the perimeter of the hatchery. The pods flapped their petals like an animal reeling in pain.

The five remaining scions charged.

"Reloading," Katan said, ejecting an empty magazine.

"Got you," Raynes said, dropping two more scions. His rifle clicked. Empty. "Reloading!"

"Got it," Katan said, popping in a fresh magazine.

A pair of scions reached the bank and hurled themselves at Halvorsen's legs, bringing her down hard against the ground. Raynes zeroed in on a scion and smashed the butt of his rifle into the back of its head. Its skull caved in like a rotten pumpkin and its body went limp. Before he could bring down the butt on his next target, a third scion reached a long, pale hand around his face while the other clamped down on his chin and pulled his face apart. The scion shoved Raynes aside, his body collapsing on the ground.

Katan aimed at the scion, took a step forward, and unloaded a full auto flurry into its midsection. Its torso ripped to shreds in a storm of flesh and bone and flames.

The last scion pounced on Halvorsen, its teeth snapping at her face while its tendrils pinned her wrists down. Katan rammed the barrel of her rifle into the back of its skull. She fired a single shot, spraying its brains into the air.

Halvorsen shoved its burning body off her and gasped a sigh of relief. Katan hauled her up. "We've gotta get the fuck out of here."

"No." Halvorsen shook her head. "We have to locate Herzog."

Katan swept a hand toward the field. The hatchery was engulfed in flames, sending stacks of heavy smoke spiraling into the jungle's canopy. "I'm pretty sure he's dead, Mia. We did all we could."

"No. We have to check the tunnel."

"Tunnel?"

Halvorsen pointed at the trench on the edge of the hatchery. A small opening about five feet high and three across framed the broad side of a rock face protruding from the ground.

"You're fucking kidding."

"You know how important this is. If he's alive he may have crucial information. We've made it this far."

Katan gritted her teeth. Fuck. She knew Halvorsen was right. They'd come this far. No point going back without knowing for sure. She nodded. "Okay."

They vaulted over the ridge of the trench. Katan crouched and shimmied through the tunnel opening. She flicked on her shoulder lamp and scanned the path for movement. After she was sure it was clear, she duck-walked across the mouth of the tunnel. Halvorsen followed close behind, her hot breath warming the back of her neck. The grooves from the mining equipment were evident as they were imprinted on the tunnel ceiling. People had been busy here. Lots of people.

The tunnel continued straight for roughly ten yards before dropping down a sloped descent. She shone her light below. There appeared to be a six-foot drop where the tunnel bottomed out. She slid down and landed on the rocky floor of a small cavern.

Katan helped Halvorsen as she dropped down. "Where the hell are we going?" Katan asked.

"Never been here. But something about this place seems unusual." She placed a palm on the wall of the cavern and pressed firmly. She pummeled the wall with the butt of her rifle. A shard of rock broke loose, scattering dust and revealing a semi-smooth surface behind it. Halvorsen shone her light on the gape. Blotches of red-orange oxidation lined portions of the wall. "Metal," she said softly.

Just ahead, the path led to the mouth of an expansive underground cave. Countless rows of thick roots dangled from the cave ceiling, all connecting to their own individual sacs, suspended just above their heads. They resembled large, fleshy bulbs, each pulsing like a heart. Every sac shared smaller, thinner shoots between themselves, like a highly complex system of electric wiring.

"Halvorsen?"

"I have no idea, Sergeant," she said, eyes wide. "These must be the organs of the pods directly above us." Halvorsen strode ahead, enchanted by their mystery. She reached out a hand, gently caressing the underbelly of a nearby pouch.

"We can't waste time," Katan said. "Let's find Herzog, and next time I promise you we'll come back with a hundred men to help you get samples. And we'll bring flamethrowers."

A strand of rootstalk broke from one of the sacks and lashed at Halvorsen. Its tendril shot up her spine and pierced the top of her head, sprouting a growth of four spindly legs. The legs clamped down on her skull like a vice, causing blood to seep down her face.

Katan quickly raised her rifle, aimed at the sac, and brought her finger to the trigger. Before she managed a shot, Halvorsen's eyes rolled back into her head as her body convulsed.

Katan gasped and took two steps backward.

Halvorsen's lips trembled. "Do. You. Speak. For. The. Flesh?"

"Mia?" Katan asked, as warm tears streamed down her cheeks.

"No."

"Who, then?" she said, jabbing the rifle in the sac's direction.

"You. Call. Us. Scion." It paused. "Am. Emissary. Of. The. Scion."

"What the fuck is going on? What do you want?"

Halvorsen's eyes rolled forward again and life streamed back into her face. The tendril jerked and manipulated her body to turn and face Katan. "Countless star cycles ago," she said, "we voyaged across the stars as you now do."

Katan surveyed the cave. The dimensions inside were strangely geometric. She recalled the metallic walls rusting behind a thin layer of rock.

"We had reached the pinnacle of our time, believing our existence to be the apex in all of creation. We were proved woefully wrong. A civilization of inorganic intelligence made contact with us and hunted us down to the point of near total annihilation."

"What the fuck are you saying?"

"The only way to survive was to remake ourselves. Avoid detection. New life. Forced evolution." Her corpse's eyes rolled into her head again.

Katan couldn't make heads or tails of the scion's story. The ludicrous image of the creature slithering into Halvorsen's brain and tinkering with her body made her want to vomit.

"We. Are. The. Planet." Halvorsen spasmed. "All. Life. Feels. Pain." Her lips snarled.

"I'm not sure what you're telling me," Katan now said, lowering her rifle. She wasn't sure if those things would ever let her leave. "What do you want from me?"

"You. Have. Brought. Technology. Pain. To. Us. You." The scion paused. "Have. Declared. War. We. Respond. Before. The. Horrors. Detect. You. And. Return." The rootstalk slithered out from under her spine. Halvorsen's body dropped to the floor.

The sacs pulsed in synchronicity, their dendrites whipping back and forth until the air hummed louder and louder, and it sounded like a swarm of wasps.

Katan sprinted for the mouth of the cave and crawled out of the tunnel.

The hatchery was now completely covered in smoke as the sky rained down torrents of ash.

Despite the heat, Katan shivered as she ran to Alpha Base, whispering a silent prayer that her father had taught her, one meant to ward off the terrors of the night. This particular terror would need more than a prayer to dispatch it, however. Soon, it would come to war.

Second Chances

The air was suffocating that night, and her curly hair became a wild, frizzy mess in that humidity. Zinnia Nieves opened her bedroom window, which overlooked southern Houston. Or what was left of it. A bright moon hung over the dark waters of the Gulf, its light glinting off the domes of the offshore chinampa cities bobbing with the tide.

The briny smell of the ocean caught on a light breeze that did little to mitigate the heat. Nearby, the roar of crashing waves bellowed like the howls of hungry monsters. Every day it seemed the water came a little closer to spilling out over the levee and swallowing a few more feet of coastline. Down the block from her apartment, the decrepit, boarded-up facades of shuttered businesses lined the street, like carrion picked clean by scavengers. She couldn't blame the people who had fled further inland. Sometimes the world felt hopeless.

Zinnia's mother had told her not to lose faith. That things would change in time. Indeed, the floating cities—which were marvels of engineering—brought promise of brighter days ahead. Sustainable gardens, safety from the elements, desalinization plants; a utopia within reach. Often, during class, Zinnia would catch herself daydreaming about living there. She longed to be under their protective bubbles. A life free of hurricanes, of government food vouchers, of nightly shootings. Though when they'd be finished being constructed was anyone's guess.

Zinnia shook the thought and returned her focus to the homework assignment at hand. She tapped a pen impatiently on her desk as she tried to think of a suitable subject to write about. She was never any good at school. Her teachers told her she couldn't hold her attention for long. It was true. Her thoughts tended to wander like dandelions in the breeze. There were days, she felt, that she was a lost cause, destined to be a loser with nothing to contribute to a society on its last legs.

She sighed, raised her tablet, and went over the prompt again. *Name a historical figure that would have continued to change the world had they not died an untimely death. And how so?* Academically, it had been a miracle she'd gotten as far as she had, but now, if she had any hopes of graduating high school, she needed to write this essay by tomorrow morning.

The walls suddenly vibrated as music played in the next room. Muffled guitars, synthesizers, accordions, bass, and drums all boomed the familiar Tejano cumbia rhythms of *Amor Prohibido.* Then came the perky voice that gave the song its soul.

It was old music. The music of her grandmother. Music Zinnia's mother now made a habit of playing every night before bed. Like many brown girls her age, Selena's voice had been a balm, a soothing escape. Her songs got her through splintered friendships, unreciprocated crushes, and those long, arduous days of summer school. On any other night, she wouldn't have minded, but with this looming deadline, she couldn't hear herself think. Zinnia pushed herself out of her chair to ask her mom to turn off the music.

Suddenly she had an epiphany.

Selena had made a considerable impact in her day. But there was always a lingering question: What if Selena's life hadn't been cut short?

What if...?

Zinnia initiated the timeline simulator app on her tablet, punched in *Selena Quintanilla Pérez*, and the program scoured the internet for pictures, video, articles; every scrap of available data pertaining to her life.

Through its use of AI software, the timeline simulator constructed a video recreation of Selena's life and upbringing. Like a movie playing in real-time, the first scene began on April 16, 1971, with the birth of Selena Quintanilla in Lake Jackson, Texas. Baby Selena cried and cooed as her mother, Marcella, nestled her in the crook of her arm. She was rendered so realistically, Zinnia thought she was looking at an actual baby.

Then came scenes of Selena's childhood days in Corpus Christi singing alongside her siblings at her father's restaurant, Papa Gayo's, or playing local parties.

"I know all this," Zinnia said, sighing. "I've seen the movie." Bored, she pressed her finger to the red timelapse bar and dragged it across the screen, fast-forwarding through Selena's early years. She skimmed over her rise to superstardom, the start of her clothing label, and her marriage to the band's guitarist, Chris Pérez.

When she released her finger, the video reached the end of Selena's timeline. March 31, 1995. The scene buffered as it rendered to life. A fragment of blurry pixels sharpened to reveal a 23-year-old Selena standing outside the door of Yolanda Saldívar's motel room at a Days Inn, her hand trembling as her fingers curled around the doorknob. A frown had been etched upon Selena's face, her brows furrowed and eyes blazing with what may have been rage or sorrow. Or both. The look of frustration marred the beautiful face Zinnia had come to know from those album covers and old concert videos. She had never seen Selena so upset. At that moment she wasn't just a celebrity, but a real, living person.

Zinnia knew what was coming and she wasn't sure she could watch what was about to unfurl, so she paused the video just before Selena opened the door. Her fingers danced on the tablet as she prompted the simulator to diverge the timeline from that point forward. It only took a few seconds for the program to calculate a new possible outcome in her life's trajectory.

Zinnia pressed the PLAY button. The scene continued and Selena entered the motel room.

"Why are you still going in there?" Zinnia said, almost pleading with Selena. Perhaps the simulator app was glitching. Selena, arms wrapped across her chest, carried on a heated conversation with Yolanda Saldívar over missing finances. Amidst tears, Selena accused Yolanda of embezzling money from her business. A shouting match erupted, and Selena turned toward the exit. Yolanda retrieved a revolver, raised her arm, and fired off a shot. Selena winced as the round struck the back of her lower right shoulder.

Zinnia gasped as Selena staggered out of the room and collapsed in the lobby, a trail of blood in her wake.

"No," said Zinnia, gasping for air. "This is all wrong." Like a drum, her heart beat furiously against her chest.

She watched as Selena was rushed to a hospital. Doctors frantically treated her wound and stopped the bleeding. The bullet had narrowly missed severing the subclavian artery, which would have proved fatal.

"Whoa," Zinnia said. She wicked a trickle of sweat from her brow with a shaking hand. She'd never witnessed something so bloody, even if it was a computer simulation. Zinnia closed her eyes, took a deep breath, and let the fire in her heart subside. When she opened her eyes again, she said, "Let's see what the future had in store for you," and skipped toward the next chapter in Selena's life.

Yolanda Saldívar was sentenced to 20 years in prison on charges of attempted murder. After her recovery, Selena took a break from recording and started a family with Chris Pérez. She gave birth to twins: a boy, Abraham, and a girl, Suzy. She named them after her brother and sister. Those early days of motherhood were filled with pride and love. As a mother, Selena was nurturing, attentive, and loving.

Zinnia found herself smiling at Selena's newfound happiness. Though there was something awfully bittersweet about being privy to moments no one had ever seen or would see. Stolen memories of a future that never was.

After two years, Selena returned to work, continuing to record new albums. She collaborated with several artists like Maná, Los Tigres del Norte, Janet Jackson, and a rising star by the name of Jennifer Lopez. In her mid-40s, she began to implement more hip-hop into her records, finding home with a new generation of fans.

Her father, Abraham, told her how proud he was of her. Selena wept tears of joy.

On many nights, Selena had confided in Chris that the gunshot wound scarring her flesh had continued to nag her, a constant reminder that she'd been fortunate to stave off death. As if she'd only temporarily eluded her true fate. There was a shadow, she'd said, hanging over her every step. Despite Chris's best efforts to comfort her, the thought kept her awake on many nights.

One summer there was a shooting at a Corpus Christi elementary school. Several children were murdered by an assailant armed with a semi-automatic assault rifle.

The horrific news broke Selena's heart. As a mother and victim of gun violence, the tragedy stirred something inside of her, a call to a higher purpose. Selena promptly announced her candidacy for mayor of Corpus Christi. Riding a wave of popularity and a platform of anti-gun violence, education, and family values, she catapulted to a landslide victory.

"You go, girl," Zinnia said propping her elbows on her desk and resting her chin between her hands.

Selena became involved in the community, becoming attentive to the needs of her constituents. Tourism soared as fans flocked just to catch a glimpse of the new mayor in action. Even immigrants and asylum seekers found haven on the streets of Corpus Christi.

After her first term as mayor, Selena leveraged her political clout into a successful run for governor of Texas, tightening gun safety laws and introducing mandatory background checks. There was a passion in Selena's eyes again, a gleam Zinnia had not seen before. There was a renewed spring in her step. The fear and guilt of being a gun violence survivor had receded and a new woman had been born of that tragedy. One with drive and purpose.

Years later, she springboarded a run for president as an independent and won a narrow victory against fellow Texan George Walker Bush. Her two terms brought about an era of prosperity. She focused on projects that stymied the effects of global climate change, like federal investments in wind and solar power, creating a reduction in greenhouse emissions. She further strengthened gun safety laws and reduced gun violence across the nation. Her government created large-scale infrastructure projects that revitalized the lifeblood of the country.

Selena's children called her their hero, and this, she told Chris, was her biggest accomplishment in life.

In the next room, *Dreaming of You* began to play. Zinnia's mother always played that ballad last just before sleep. It was late. Outside, the stars glimmered like gems in the sky. Zinnia felt her eyes grow heavy. She thought about turning off the tablet, but felt a compulsion to know everything, to see Selena through. She owed her that much.

Zinnia fast-forwarded again. On July 10th, 2032, toward the end of her second presidential term, Selena had been touring the scene of a deadly tornado disaster in Williamson County, Texas, meeting and greeting the residents affected by the devastation. A local man incensed with her gun laws, approached her, pulled a gun from his waistband, and shot her dead at the age of 61.

Warm tears pooled in Zinnia's eyes as she stared blankly at the tablet. When she finally blinked, her tears cascaded down her cheeks and plopped onto the screen. Like a black hole, a painful, profound wound opened in her heart.

The following night, her fans held vigils all over the country: the Lincoln Memorial, Times Square, Sunset Boulevard, the streets of Corpus Christi. Seas of candles lit the night like stars in the sky.

Zinnia paused the video and tried to stifle her sobs, but it was useless. She buried her head between her hands and wept until her eyes became puffy. It couldn't be. The shadow that had hung over Selena's life had finally caught up to her. She wanted to curse the universe. Was a person's fate unavoidable?

She wiped her tears with the back of her hand. The song next door wound down, leaving the world in silence. She didn't know why she felt the way she had over a virtual ghost whose fictive life had been distilled into a collection of simulated bits and pixels. In only a short span, she'd come to know Selena in a way no one ever would.

Zinnia inhaled a breath of humid air and composed herself, sitting there until curiosity began to gnaw at her. She had to know: What kind of a world did Selena leave behind? Zinnia prompted the simulator to leap ahead one last time.

She jumped several years ahead into that alternate future. A new scene began to render, and she gasped as she beheld great domed cities lining the rust-colored surface of Mars. There was an old woman dressed in ceremonial garb standing in front of a great hall. She had familiar brown eyes and wild, curly hair. She wore a warm smile as she greeted a crowd of newly arrived Terran refugees.

"I know on Earth your homes and dreams have washed away," the woman said. "But here on Mars, we are all entitled to a second chance. Welcome."

An old man approached her and held her hand tenderly. "Gracias, Presidente Nieves."

Smiling, Zinnia turned off the program and glanced out her window. The moon had slunk away, and the hints of a new sun began to paint the sky as it peeked over the eastern waters. The chinampa cities became clear in that golden light, their promise brighter than ever.

Whether fate was unavoidable, she couldn't know. But perhaps the echoes of good deeds still found their way rippling into futures yet unwritten.

The sunlight caught on her desk. She still had a few hours before class. Zinnia Nieves switched on her tablet and began to type up her report.

The Incident at Chicxulub

Outside his home, on the sloped streets above Chicxulub, Felix looked down on the tranquil waters of its port. For years, on any given summer day, the Mexican Gulf would've been a bustling source of commerce, but on this day the fishing boats sat idle, their reflections motionless in the waning afternoon light. The docks had been emptied for weeks now and not a single fisherman scurried about their weathered planks.

He'd heard the fishermen say the ocean had become too warm in the last few years and the fish had died or left for colder waters. All he knew was that the town had been hungry and left wanting for money which would not arrive. His mother was the town curandera. He had asked her once if she could draw on the power of the gods and heal the people, make the pain in their tummies go away, or pray for wealth and good fortune. She said it didn't work like that. The gods, she said, had left mortals to deal with mortal issues.

Felix shook his head and cursed the gods under his breath. What good were they?

His mother peered through the door of their house, rubbing her pendant between her thumb and forefinger. "Mijo, dinner is almost ready," she said, her voice low and tired. "Can you stop by the grocer and pick up two loaves of bread?"

"Si, Mamá," he said.

She handed him a scrunched-up hundred-peso bill.

"We don't have much money left," she said. "The bread will have to last us the whole week."

Felix nodded and strode past the shuttered artisan stalls, the rundown homes, and the old church. There, wandering the narrow streets, walked a lanky middle-aged gringo. His pale face snickered as he looked about town, wincing at the dust that seemed to linger in the air far too long for his liking. As he patted the dirt off his suit, he noticed Felix.

"You. Boy," the man said. "Come here. Ven aqui."

Felix looked around. The streets were barren. Most people had probably gone home for the day. He shuffled toward the man slowly, timidly.

"My name is Professor Frederick Lamont," the man said bending over to match Felix's eye level. "I'm here on an important archeological study on behalf of Miskatonic University. Who might you be, chap?"

"My name is Felix."

"Felix, you look like a nice boy. I'm looking for an old book said to be located in this very town. A thick, worn manuscript that chronicled the town's history. Perhaps you know the one of which I speak?"

Felix said nothing.

Lamont eyed the crumpled bill in Felix's hand.

"I, of course," Lamont said pulling a money clip from his back pocket, "can offer you money for information regarding its whereabouts." He slid out a wad of cash. "I've heard fishing's been awful around these parts this year. No business."

Felix licked his lips. He knew his mother could use the money.

"I think I know," Felix said. "I heard it's located in the church, but no one is allowed to see it besides the priest who keeps it safe."

Lamont smirked. "Ah, now we're getting somewhere." He extended his hand out to Felix, offering him the money. Before Felix could grasp it, Lamont snapped his hand back. "In my hand I hold two hundred dollars. It's yours if you fetch me the book."

Felix swallowed and shook his head. "My mother told me that book is sacred. I would get in trouble."

"Is your family hungry, Felix? Wouldn't you like to help your mother? Think of how happy she'd be when you show her this money," he said, waving the cash.

Felix turned toward the church. It sat old and worn, its white paint flaking, revealing layers of moldy wood underneath.

His stomach rumbled. He looked upon the tattered bill in his hand. "Yes," Felix said. "I can get it for you."

Felix's sandals slapped against the cobblestone path that snaked its way from the heart of town all the way to its rotting, crumbling docks. His legs burned, as if his muscles had been doused in petrol and set ablaze. Taking the book had proven easy enough. Not being spotted had been another matter. He looked frantically around for the man in the evening's waning light. At the tip of the dock, Frederick Lamont flicked his cigarette into the still waters of the Mexican Gulf.

The professor waited with crossed arms, his fine leather shoes tapping impatiently on the plank floors. Behind him, the sky grew dark.

Felix handed him the old tome and bent over to catch his breath. "It was locked in the belfry. I pried the key from the priest's drawer."

"Did anyone see you, boy?" Lamont asked.

"Yes," Felix said gasping. He turned toward town. The chorus of voices began to rise in the distance like the buzzing of angry hornets. "The priest saw me take the codex."

"Damn," Lamont said through gritted teeth.

Felix braced both hands together. "Can I have my money, sir?"

"There's no time." Lamont began flipping through the book's tattered pages, biting down on his lip until a small sliver of blood trickled down his chin.

"What's so important about that book?" Felix said.

"Don't you know your own town's history?" Lamont said, as his eyes darted madly across the pages.

Felix shrugged. "My mamá says that book is never to be read or discussed."

"That's why you and your ilk will remain ignorant and subservient to people like me. Because you don't understand the very treasures you have under your very feet."

Felix said nothing. Lamont offered the boy a quick glimpse and pursed his lips.

"I suppose I can tell you a little secret," he said smiling, tracing his fingers through lines of faded text. "Long ago, a Spanish galleon sank in these waters. Only one person survived. This lone sailor swam back to town and relayed his story to the local priest, who transcribed his account into this very codex."

The drone of angry voices drew nearer, filling the streets behind them.

Lamont continued. "The sailor's account described an enormous creature that rose from the depths, bearing the tentacled face of an octopus and the body of a humanoid man. It sprouted mammoth wings from its back, which it wrathfully flapped about, causing a tempest to capsize the ship."

"Like a Mayan god?" Felix asked.

Lamont shook his head, his eyes never breaking from the book. "It's not some silly jungle myth, boy. I think we're dealing with something tangible. Something alien and powerful."

A crowd of villagers marched down the road, their steps and shouts unifying into a maddening cacophony.

Lamont began flipping through the book indiscriminately, creasing its pages and ripping away threads of stitched binding. "We stand on the very site of a large-scale global event. We are in the heart of the Chicxulub crater, where a celestial body crashed into the Earth sixty-six million years ago. It wiped out nearly all life on the planet, but I know it wasn't just some asteroid."

The priest stepped onto the docks, the townsfolk marching behind him. They waved machetes and torches angrily in the air.

Felix felt beads of sweat accumulating on his head. "Sir, I think I'm going to get in trouble. I see my mamá coming. Can I just have my money now?"

Lamont grimaced as his fingers raked across the book, flipping page after page. "The sailor made mention to the priest the beast's name, which it repeatedly bellowed out before killing the crew. I must find its name so that I may call it. To call it is to unleash its power. To unleash its power is to in essence become a god." He looked up at Felix, his eyes now bursting with broken blood vessels. Felix stepped back. Lamont jabbed his finger on the book, drool seeping from the corner of his mouth. "I've found it! By God, I've found it!"

"Don't proceed any further," the priest said, wrapping an arm around Felix, gently nudging him behind his own body. Felix's mother quickly approached and pulled him toward her, her wrinkled face frowning, scolding him with a fury no words could ever convey.

"You're all too late," Lamont said. He turned toward the Gulf's waters and closed his eyes. "K'utulu! K'utulu! K'utulu!"

The earth trembled, sending some of the townsfolk tumbling into the water. Felix slipped, slamming his head on the planks of the dock. The waters began to bubble like soup in a pot. A few hundred yards from the dock, a large monster sprang from the ocean, towering over the entire town like a small mountain.

Lamont raised his arms. "Rise, Lord K'utulu. Set your eyes upon me, that I am your master."

The beast opened its eyes. Like fiery embers, they were filled with rage. Countless tentacles writhed along its mouth as it shrieked in anger. It opened its leathery wings, which were akin to those of a bat.

"Mireya," the priest said, looking at Felix's mother. "The church has no power here. It is time for the real gods, curandera."

Felix's mother nodded and raised her arms to the heavens. She chanted hushed words in a language he couldn't understand, as if uttering some ancient secret to the wind.

Then the sky cracked with thunder and a burst of fire lit the sky.

The crowd pointed upward and gasped. There, a feathered serpent descended from the heavens like a shooting star.

"Kukulkan!" the people shouted in unison.

Felix recognized the name. Kukulkan, the great Mayan god.

The serpent uncoiled itself, revealing its true size. Felix surmised it spanned the length of a great, winding river. Just that instant, Kukulkan's eyes settled on the water beast. The snake god's lips curled, fangs protruding as it hissed.

K'utulu roared and clawed at the air in response.

The people cried and sprinted back toward town.

"Come," Felix's mother said, "we must go." She squeezed his hand and led him away from the dock.

K'utulu stamped a leg into the waters. The world quaked and the ocean erupted.

Kukulkan closed its wings and dove downward like a spear. The feathered serpent struck K'utulu in the chest with its head, knocking the monster backward a few paces.

K'utulu shrieked and regained its balance. It then countered with a clawed slash to the serpent's face. Rivers of blood seeped from Kukulkan, flowing into the blue waters below.

Lamont shouted incoherently while prancing about, his shoes tapping madly on the docks. "Your old jungle gods can't save you people! The world is mine for the taking!"

K'utulu stepped forward and clutched Kukulkan in a constricting embrace, its dozen slithering tentacles wrapping themselves around the Mayan god's neck. Kukulkan writhed in what Felix perceived to be excruciating pain.

His mother bowed her head and whispered into the pendant around her neck. The words flew from her mouth in that cryptic, ancient language.

Kukulkan's tail slithered up K'utulu's face and slashed his opponent's eye. K'utulu released its grasp on the god, stumbling backward as it howled.

As it wailed, the great Mayan god quickly embedded its fangs into K'utulu's neck and pierced its tail through its heart, silencing the beast for good.

K'utulu's one good eye rolled behind its massive head. Its body fell backwards into the Gulf, shooting a geyser of water into the air. The shockwave rolled through the docks, splintering the wood in a mighty explosion that cast Lamont into the depths of the sea, the codex alongside him.

Lamont gasped, reaching for the remnants of the dock with outstretched arms but K'utulu's sinking corpse created a whirlpool that sucked the man deep into the dark abyss below.

Kukulkan shot forth from the ocean and flew back into the heavens, vanishing into the darkness of the night.

After a while, the waves began to sway gently, until they became still, and silence filled Chicxulub once more. The townsfolk gazed appreciatively upon the sky before turning home.

Felix's mother placed a soft hand on his shoulder as she led him back to town.

"There are secrets, mijo," she said to him at last, "that have more value locked away in the depths of our hearts, than do all the riches in the world secured in our palms."

Felix held her hand and nodded. It would be a lesson he knew he would never forget.

The Revolution Engine

Miguel Montez wiped the sweat from his brow and hoisted open the garage door. The sun hadn't yet appeared above the horizon, and already he felt its heat rising from the cobblestone streets. The light crept inside the garage and lit the skeletal remains of what used to be automobiles. Splayed out across his workspace were spare parts, broken motors, and an old chassis that looked like a crushed can of sardines.

They were all long-term projects; parts were hard to come by in this part of the world. But it kept him busy, and it kept him sane. He was the town's mechanic when he wasn't working at the petrol refinery a few miles south of town. Today was his first day off in a week.

The streets of Samalayuca, Mexico were made of cracked stone, and the few homes that still stood were of old adobe. The town was surrounded by the infamous dunes of the Samalayuca Desert and lay a few miles south of the New Mexico border. It wasn't so much a town as it was a bone-dry community of ranchers, and laborers who toiled in the refinery.

Miguel walked inside the garage. A few dark blotches of gangly legs crept back from the light and scuttled into the cracks and crevices of the shadows. He brushed dust off the generator and cranked the handle ten times. The electricity hummed as it coursed through the veins of the old building. The lights came on and the radio cackled its white noise. Miguel twisted the dial a few degrees to the right and homed in on the town's only station. The voice was that of Felipe Cazares, a janitor at the refinery. His hobby wasn't so much the radio as it was hearing himself talk. Today he was rambling on about the Cold War between Soviet communists and the capitalist Americans.

Communism: it was an ideal that had caught like wildfire since the war. The basic principle was that the good of the community outweighed the good of the individual. Prosperity in numbers. What's good for all is good for the one, and so on. The government basically fostered a state where no one would go for wanting and everything would be provided, given that everyone pulled their share of labor. It was a concept that overtook the poor, and in Mexico, the idea had latched on like a common street-alley flea.

Miguel had no interest in politics. It was all bickering and nonsensical banter over how to fix this or that. Now, mechanical engineering was something he could get behind. You only fixed something when you put in the work. And the answer was always the same. If a tire went flat, you changed it; if a timing belt snapped, you replaced it; if something needed alignment, you adjusted accordingly. No debating, no smoke-blowing, just elbow grease and resolve.

He lit a cigarette, inhaling smoke and dust. He walked past the wrecked cars and into his office. A stack of unpaid bills hung on the edge of his desk. There were no letters from back home today. It had been five months since he'd heard from his family in San Diego. Mail traveled slowly in the arid parts of northern Mexico, and sometimes never at all. He scratched at his two-day-old beard and rolled up his sleeves. The Marine Corps tattoo was stamped on his forearm like a badge of honor. It felt like a lifetime ago.

He grabbed his torch and strapped on his goggles. He lit the pilot with his cigarette and started to weld the broken chassis of an old pre-war Ford truck; it was so battered he couldn't be sure what year it rolled out of the assembly line.

He guided the flame along the edge of the new plates he'd installed along the doors. Sparks flew like fireworks and cooled on the floor. A knock came at the door. Miguel took off his goggles and killed the flame.

Ramiro Bravo, the foreman at the refinery, stood clutching his hat, his veins nearly bursting out of his fists. He was nervous. He was not the type to get nervous, and that made Miguel uneasy.

"Hello, Miguel," said Bravo. "We are having an emergency meeting at the refinery. I would very much like for you to join us."

"What's this about?"

"I think it will be better to say once we are all gathered."

"Who is *we*?"

"The entire town, Miguel. It concerns all of us."

Bravo smiled and left to pester the next adobe over. Miguel lit another cigarette, took a drag, and stomped it out. He closed shop and joined the line of villagers already walking toward the refinery; like a line of ants along the dusty streets, they marched.

⁂

He saw his co-workers: Marco Torres, Enrique Ortega, Julio Paz, Felipe Cazares. Even people from town like Father Camacho and Cesar Maldivia, the most important rancher in Samalayuca. All the wives of the workers were there, some holding infants in their arms, shielding them from leaking drops of water that came from somewhere in the rafters.

They gathered in the open clearing of the plant floor. They were surrounded by leaky pipes and steam. Father Camacho pulled out a handkerchief and wiped the sweat from his eyes.

Ramiro Bravo walked forward, holding a piece of paper.

"Thank you for coming. I will get to the point, as time is of the essence. I received a telegram this morning from the Head of the Armed Forces in the capital. Ladies and gentlemen, last night Soviet forces launched a rapid reconnaissance force. They landed on the Port of Veracruz and are aiming to bypass our forces to establish a foothold on the southern United States border. The Mexican army hasn't had enough time to mobilize, and the Reds are on a path for Samalayuca."

"Why here? There is nothing here," said Cesar Maldivia.

"Because," Bravo sighed, "we have a crucial refinery that would help establish a fueling depot for any oncoming Soviet forces. The Soviet Union has launched a preemptive strike on our neighbors to the north, and we are unfortunately at their mercy."

Miguel saw as the women clutched their babies tighter. The chatter broke out and the words flew like a swarm of locusts.

"When are they due to arrive?" asked Miguel.

Bravo looked at the telegram. His frown curved his mustache downward. "Within one day."

"Well, what are we waiting for? We have to evacuate," said Marco Torres, one of the tanker drivers. "We can drop the fuel loads and attach an empty cargo hitch to load up some of the people on a flatbed. Cesar, maybe you could spare some of your horses . . ."

"I'm afraid that won't be an option," Bravo cut in. "The Mexican government has ordered that we do what we can to stop or slow their advance. We are the only line of defense. If they find we have fled, they will round up the deserters and execute us."

The refinery became silent.

Father Camacho ran a trembling hand along his hair. "Perhaps we can negotiate with them? I believe some of the people in town are sympathetic to their cause . . ."

"No chance, Father. They have no God. The state is their God," said Maldivia. "They have forsaken their principles for a lust for power."

"Miguel, that's where I was hoping you'd come in. I know you've fought in the war," Bravo said.

The crowd of about fifty turned to him.

"That was over ten years ago. Besides, we don't have any weapons that could touch theirs," Miguel said. This couldn't be happening. He looked around. He wasn't born in Mexico. He was born in San Diego, California. He knew the luxury of the ocean, a good meal, and steady work. He knew hope. They didn't. The skinny, tanned souls looked to him; not their priest, or the foreman, but him.

Miguel sighed. "I can make some suggestions. But first we need to find a safe place for the women and children."

"I can take them to my ranch, there would be plenty of room," said Maldivia.

"No," Miguel said. "They would expect the ranch to be a rallying point for a possible resistance. It's a strong candidate for a shelling. The safest place would be the refinery."

The women gasped.

"I know it seems counterintuitive, but this place is a commodity. They wouldn't risk shelling this place. They can go down to the basement levels. We'll shut off the pipeline before they get here. They won't be able to tap into the petrodiesel right away, and the families will be safer."

"Ortega, Paz, Luna," Bravo said, "take the women and children downstairs. Get them water and hard hats. Ladies, these gentlemen will take you down; your children will be safe there."

The women and the children made their way down. Miguel thought about home. He doubted he'd have enough time to draw up a letter for his family. Besides, there would be no one to deliver mail for a few weeks. Miguel thought about his mother back home. He prayed his brothers were taking good care of her.

"Now, what weapons do we have?" asked Miguel.

"I have a few revolvers in my house," said Bravo. "I know Luna has a shotgun. Maldivia?"

Maldivia rubbed his chin. "I have a cache at the ranch. About a dozen rifles, six revolvers, and a box of dynamite from my old mining days."

Miguel nodded. "It's a start. We can't win a direct firefight. During the war, I fought in the Battle of Garapan, in the Pacific Theater. The Japanese practiced guerilla warfare in the streets, shooting from the pockets of rubble, behind the windows of homes and temples. We have to do the same. Maldivia, you have a ranch, you must have traps."

"Yes, I use bear traps to stop coyotes and mountain lions from getting to my horses."

"We'll need all of them. And all your horses. Round up everything you can. Take what men you need and meet back in town in four hours."

Maldivia nodded, picked out a dozen men, and ran off.

"Miguel, everyone else, please come with me," said Bravo.

They walked to the elevator. The men put on their hard hats and crammed into the rusty cage.

"I know some of the men know the legends, but Miguel, have you heard of Pancho Villa?" Bravo pulled a key that was tied around his neck. He inserted the key into a slot by the elevator door.

"He was a freedom fighter, right?" Miguel said.

"He was a revolutionary fighter who challenged the dictatorship of President Porfirio Diaz in 1910." The elevator lurched downward, creaking and shifting occasionally. "Under Porfirio's rule, industry boomed, and modernization approached at rapid speeds, at the expense of human rights and liberal reforms. Everyone who opposed him was crushed under the wheels of his reign."

"Yeah, and?"

"Villa was known for occasionally crossing the border and raiding American trains for supplies and weapons. In January, 1916, he raided an American train near Santa Isabel, Chihuahua. This caused the United States to begin a manhunt for him that lasted years. They never did apprehend him, but what is never mentioned is why the Americans were so intent on his capture. Truth is this: Villa and his men detached a car from the end of that train. In it they found an incredible piece of technology: a tank that hovered above ground. It is believed the Americans were sending it to the Nationalist Army to crush the rebellion."

"That sounds impossible. Why hasn't anyone heard of it?"

"Because no one knew how to operate it. Villa transported the tank to Samalayuca, where it could be kept secret. The Mexican Revolution continued for a few more years and Villa was assassinated by his fellow men. The tank was forgotten by the Mexicans, and the Americans declined to confirm its existence. But it is here, in our facilities, in a secret subterranean level."

The elevator shook and came to a stop. The heat was almost unbearable, and Miguel had a hard time breathing. The men got off the lift and stared at a blue tarp over a large, bulky frame.

"Miguel, this has been one of the greatest kept secrets of the Revolution. To date, this technology has not been replicated anywhere in the world."

Bravo walked to the blue mass and removed the tarp.

An olive-green monstrosity of ironwork and gears stared back in its mechanical slumber. It had long tracks like the standard M2 tank he'd operated during the war, but on each side of the frame was attached a large-bladed turbine, which Miguel presumed would shift underneath the tank to propel it upward. A long cannon and a Gatling gun turret protruded from the top.

The men oohed and ahed.

"What does it run on?" asked Miguel.

"Petrodiesel," smiled Bravo. "It's a simple piston combustion engine. We believe whoever built it wanted advanced technology that could be easy to maintain. Something any grease monkey could fix. Only thing is the company that runs the refinery never wanted to risk driving it for fear of crashing it. Now we have no choice. Miguel, do you think you can give it a spin?" He took off another key from around his neck and handed it to Miguel.

Miguel walked to the tank. He touched its smooth surface. He felt the dormant power that awaited inside. It was an intimidating piece of technology: something from another world, something that shouldn't have even existed. The U.S. military hadn't even had anything like this during his time there over a decade ago. He climbed a set of rusted rungs that led him to the hatch. He opened the iron dome and climbed inside. It was confined and hot and the view slit was smaller than he'd liked. It felt like being in a tin can; it was like being home again.

The real surprise was that the controls were basically the same layout as his M2. He inserted his key into the ignition and the beast roared alive. He could hear the gears clanking and the pistons hammering away. He manipulated the levers, and the tracks turned the machine left. He switched the levers, and the machine pivoted right. Cake.

A blue lever sat in between his legs. He pulled it back and the tracks came together, shifted to the rear of the tank, and turned so that the tank looked like a cross. The turbines on the side came together underneath the belly of the tank and blew a torrent of hot air at the concrete floor like a roaring dragon.

The tank hovered six feet off the ground. The same levers that steered the tracks shifted the angles of the turbines. He steered as easily as if he had been piloting the machine for years.

He pushed the blue lever back and the formation readjusted itself to standard settings. He hopped off the tank and stared at his coworkers, their hardhats spilled on the floor.

His eyes gleamed as a fire coursed through his veins. "I think I have an idea."

All the men gathered on the roof of Miguel's garage. The sun had just set below the dunes to the west and the first hints of a purple sky came to greet them.

Miguel spent the last hours of sunlight drawing up a plan. Part of that plan included creating makeshift weapons and finishing up his pet truck project. He rounded up every welding torch he could find and connected aluminum hoses to small diesel tanks and made flamethrowers for some of the men.

They were all armed. Alonzo Luna with his shotgun and large Bowie knife; Ramiro Bravo with his dual revolvers tucked inside his holsters; Cesar Maldivia with his rifle and bandolier strapped across his chest; Felipe Cazares with his hardhat and sticks of dynamite tied around his body; Marco Torres and Enrique Ortega with their welding goggles and flamethrowers. Even the men without firearms came equipped with wrenches and machetes. It was as if an old Mexican revolutionary army enlisted a band of grease monkeys to do the fighting.

Miguel looked south toward the refinery. It was empty, save for the yucca shrubs and a few scattered pronghorns galloping toward hazy horizons.

"Why did you come here, Montez?" asked Father Camacho, armed only with a wooden cross around his neck.

Miguel looked at the refinery. It was a gamble leaving the women there, but with any luck the distraction would work. "It wasn't by choice. I was deported."

"That explains your accent."

Miguel smiled. "I was born in California. I fought in the 2nd Tank Battalion for the Marine Corps during the second World War. I bled for my country, and they tossed me out like I was a foreigner."

"Well, you are one of us now. No matter what happens, we are glad to call you brother."

"Amen!" shouted Julio Paz. Cesar Maldivia slapped a hand on Miguel's shoulder. The rest of the twenty men cheered atop their lungs. Their cries echoed across the desert, scattering small birds into the sky.

A small rumble shifted loose sand on the adobe roof. The men looked at the southern horizon. The unified hum of distant motors grew louder. In the sky, a dark sphere approached. It was a scout zeppelin. As it approached, the details grew clear: it was a dark metallic grey, with a giant red insignia bearing a hammer and a scythe. It turned its spotlight on as it neared the refinery.

"Damn," said Miguel under his breath. "I didn't think they'd have one of those. If we could shoot out the spotlight, we'd neutralize their eye in the sky."

"Are you sure? Can it retaliate?" asked Bravo.

"They won't have any weapons on that thing; any misfire and the zeppelin goes up in flames, causing a big risk for the ground units when it comes crashing down."

"I'll ride out on my fastest horse and shoot out the spotlight before it gets to town," said Maldivia.

"Alright. You remember the plan?"

"Yes, amigo. I'll see you soon. Viva la revolución!"

Maldivia climbed down the ladder and mounted his horse. He took off toward the refinery at full gallop.

"Alright, now remember the plan, gentlemen: the Reds are going to come to secure the town. We are going to hit them from every nook and cranny. Everyone mind the bear traps and remember where to drop the dynamite. Lead them toward the dunes and wait for my command."

The men slid down the ladder and took their positions. Some waited by darkened windows; others took refuge in the openings of wells; others propped chairs and tables by their homes for cover.

The zeppelin gleamed in the distance. The horizon grew dark blue. The light in the sky probed the earth like an evil eye. It flew about two miles from town. A trickle of sweat found its way streaming down Miguel's head. He realized it wasn't the heat—the air had cooled as a desert breeze blew in—but nervousness, making him sweat. If the light found the men, their plan would blow away like leaves in a storm.

He looked around. The men gripped their rifles and licked their lips. The light touched the first row of homes, casting long shadows on the streets. Ortega pushed his back against the wall of the town bar. The spotlight hovered over the roof and was about to find its first man when it suddenly went out in a burst of sparks.

Miguel knew the next step and it would be the most frightening: the shelling would soon commence. And like an answer from the devil himself, the first shell whistled ominously above the night sky. He closed his eyes and prayed. It's all anybody could do.

The bomb struck the town square, obliterating the market and post office. Everything after that was a blur. It was like being in the middle of a lightning storm, and everything was getting hit.

He wasn't sure if it was twenty minutes or an hour, but the shelling eventually stopped. The smell of burning wood and thick smoke filled Miguel's lungs. He could hear the others coughing and spitting.

The air went still and cold. The fires crackled and danced atop the buildings.

Engines roared in the distance. Miguel hoped the men held their fire until the Reds were in the streets. He ran to the northern edge of town where the hovertank sat in darkness. He climbed to the top to get a vantage point over the scene. He waited.

The first line of Soviet soldiers walked out of the darkness and into the streets. There were about twenty of them, and they wore light-grey uniforms with red insignias. They looked like they were cut out of the same mold as they marched in uniformity. Half a dozen tanks followed slowly in a line. Another thirty men crept behind the tanks as they peered into broken windows.

After the flow of soldiers stopped, the first attack came. The dynamite exploded, hitting the first line of men. Limbs flew everywhere, slamming into walls, into the church, into the cantina. The fallen soldiers slowed the advance of the tanks and the men behind them.

The men of Samalayuca rushed out of hiding and opened a volley. The air cracked with gunfire as rifles and revolvers laid into the Russian troops. The soldiers returned fire with automatic rifles and machine guns. Some Mexicans fell from rooftops, and if the gunshots didn't kill them, the fall broke their necks.

Thunder and smoke filled the streets as bullets flew. Both sides fired vulgarities neither understood.

Miguel thought he spotted Luna taking a few potshots at the Red infantry with his shotgun from the steps of the church. After a while Miguel lost sight of him.

Once the fighting was underway, the Firemen had their cue. They had waited to spring on the Red Army from behind. Miguel saw Torres break a window with his elbow as a stream of diesel fuel sprayed the soldiers' backs, followed swiftly by a burst of flame. The soldiers who were coated in flames ran in every direction. Those who strayed toward the side streets triggered the iron jaws of the bear traps. They lay screaming on the dirt roads, maimed and in flames.

The tanks aimed their cannons at the buildings. In a flash, rubble and fire erupted everywhere. The soldiers spilled into every house, rushing in like fire ants. He knew his men had no chance in a close quarter confrontation.

As his eyes scoured the battlefield, Miguel saw less and less of his compatriots. The remaining few gathered on the western edge of town and fought backward toward the dark of the dunes.

The Soviets pushed forward. The infantry laid covering fire as the tanks gave chase into the dunes.

The tanks had trouble gaining traction over the shifting sands. Miguel noted the sharp temperature drop, strapped on his goggles, and closed the hatch. He began his advance.

Mexicans and Russians exchanged fire in the chilling desert air. The infantry closed in on the surviving townsfolk as their tanks lagged behind. As the fighting grew feverish, the tank engines sputtered and stalled. The iron beasts coughed and gurgled as if in their death throes. The tanks stopped running.

At that moment, an explosive shot pierced the armor of a Soviet tank, barraging nearby men with shrapnel.

A war cry rang out from behind the Soviet Army. From the darkness, a green tank rushed forward, hovering above the sands on two large turbines. A cavalry of townsfolk armed with rifles and flamethrowers followed close behind. Maldivia led the mounted men with a rifle held to the sky, like an offering to the gods of revolution.

The Soviet turrets remained frozen in place as Miguel shelled them one by one. Their armored innards exploded, and the few survivors spilled out of the tanks in screams.

The hovertank maneuvered smoothly, shifting side to side over men and sand dunes, deflecting machine gun fire. The mounted villagers surrounded the Soviet infantry, setting stragglers ablaze. As Miguel's hovertank neared, it blew sand skyward, creating a miniature sandstorm. The battlefield became a haze of flames, sand, and gunfire.

The gears of the hovertank sputtered and creaked. Miguel clutched at the levers and pulled as hard as he could. It rattled violently as gunfire ricocheted off its body. The hovertank crashed down, and the turbines cracked under the weight of the iron beast.

He banged his head against the command console and the world started to fade. The last thing he heard was a loud blast. Then, the world went dark.

⁓

The moisture on his face woke him. He'd dreamt that he was drowning. He reached for his face and felt sweat. His fingers probed a cut across his right eye where scar tissue had formed. When Miguel opened his eyes, he was staring at the ceiling of the Samalayuca Catholic Church. He tried to stand, but his body ached. He felt a hand under his back gently lifting him up. He turned to see Father Camacho smiling.

"Father, how long was I out?"

"Only a few hours, Miguel. Come, I want you to see this."

Father Camacho gently helped Miguel to his feet. Miguel rubbed his temples as his head pounded.

"What happened, Father? Did the plan work?"

Camacho said nothing as he guided Miguel toward the door.

As Miguel looked around, he saw most of the stained-glass windows shattered as the church was awash in sunlight. Motes of dust hung in the air like a desert snowfall.

The wooden doors to the church were unhinged and leaning at an angle, possibly knocked loose from the shock of a nearby shell.

Waiting for him on the steps were a dozen men. Some with varying degrees of wounds, but all stained with blood.

He saw Julio Paz without a rifle, but his Bowie knife was tucked in his belt, bloodied and as worn as its owner.

There was Maldivia, the rancher strapped with an empty bandolier and a hearty smile.

Marco Torres flashed a smirk as he pulled back his tinted goggles. His face was covered in soot.

The rest of the men were ranchers or refinery workers he hadn't had the pleasure of knowing too well.

He didn't see Enrique Ortega or Felipe Cazares. Gone was Alonzo Luna, as was his boss Ramiro Bravo, the man who gifted him the hovertank.

As Miguel's eyes adjusted to the sun, he finally saw it: the full force of American military might. A line of mechanized warfare advanced in a single formation that ran through the town and staged by the refinery. A battalion of hovertanks swept through the stone streets, blowing debris and sand into the air. To the east and west, crab-shaped armored vehicles with protruding cannons walked across the dunes, surveying their surroundings with a strange curiosity. A line of men in green uniforms marched by with proud, stoic faces. Up in the clouds, a platoon of blue zeppelins patrolled the horizon beyond the refinery.

"Wh-what happened?"

"We won, Miguel," said Maldivia, "Your plan worked. We surrounded their infantry, and they soon surrendered. Their tanks were immobilized just as you predicted. And the women, I am glad to say, are safe."

"We did it? We held back the Soviet Army?"

"Yes, amigo, we won," Maldivia said, with a smile that curved his mustache upward. "The Mexican army got in touch with the Americans and is now working on a joint counter-offensive to drive back the Soviets from our shores. We denied them a foothold last night."

Miguel shook his head. He couldn't believe it.

"I must ask, Miguel. How did you know their tanks would break down?"

"Well, I assumed that since the Soviets wanted access to our refinery, they used petrodiesel as a fuel source. The thing about that is we use paraffin wax in the fuel blend to keep other components and chemicals from separating from the petrol. At 30 degrees Celsius, the wax begins to separate from the diesel, which then coats fuel filters and clogs them with a gunky buildup. Without the wax, the water in the diesel begins to freeze and the fuel takes on a gelatinous state. Samalayuca boasts a very hot desert during the day, and an equally cold one at night. I knew if we could lure them into the dunes not only would they lose traction, but I knew it would be a matter of time before their engines stalled."

Maldivia nodded and the rest of the men smiled.

Torres looked at the crab tanks to the east, raising a hand to shield his eyes from the sun. "I didn't know your people had this technology at their disposal. I've never seen anything like it."

"You're right; they've come a long way. We're looking at an entirely new era, Torres. I'm guessing those machines run on atomic engines. But you're wrong about one thing: those aren't my people. My people are standing right in front of me."

He embraced them as he looked at the metallic monoliths treading across the sands. The fires dwindled, and the smoke snaked around the tattered buildings. And as Miguel looked west, the always shifting sands of the dunes had already begun swallowing the Soviet tanks. The hovertank, too, was now out of sight, lost forever to the earth beneath their feet.

And south, the machines of the new world, powered by the atom, assembled. The dawn of a new era, indeed. The dawn of another World War fast approached.

Calypso and the Kami

Calypso heard the two men whispering by the side of the track while she readied herself on the mark. Her feet pressed against the cinder blocks and she felt them give way against the soil. The white lines on the track had faded into the earth, leaving only faint, dull stripes and pockmarked patches of dirt and dead grass where the men played soccer on the weekends.

Two boys who had been kicking a ball around the field stopped to stare at her. They pulled their eyelids back and waddled about, giggling. She turned away and pushed them out of her mind. Sitting on the bleachers, she observed a few men, women, and children scattered about, most of them wearing strange clothing and loose, colorful garments. Their eyes were fixed on her, unblinking, unmoving.

"Aiko Tanaka," the man in the trilby hat said, scribbling on his clipboard.

"Calypso," Coach Benitez said. "She doesn't like to be called Aiko."

The man nodded his head. "And her father was Japanese born, am I correct?"

"That's right, both her parents were Japanese. She was born here in Peru, though."

"Does she know?"

"Not yet. She lives in the slums outside of Lima, so there's not much by way of television. Even periodicals can be hard to come by. I'm sure if all goes well, the good news will help soften the blow."

"Right," the man said forcing a smile. "Let's see what she's got."

"Okay, Calypso," Coach Benitez said, turning to her. He winked and nodded, flashing the same warm smile of encouragement that had gotten so many kids through the long track seasons in Lima. "Let's show this man how fast you can run." He raised the whistle to his lips and blew.

She pushed off the cinder blocks and bolted toward the 100-meter line. The wind lashed across her face as her muscles expanded and contracted, one leg after the other, her heart beating against her chest. As she approached the finish line, her right foot landed on a small stone and her ankle rolled. She felt a strange pop in her bones.

Calypso tumbled along the dirt, her arms burning until she skidded to a dead stop. She screamed as the fire in her ankle pulsed to the beat of her pumping heart.

She pushed herself off the ground and hopped off the track. The people in the bleachers stared, unmoving, unconcerned.

Coach Benitez ran up to her, resting a gentle hand on her shoulder.

"Calypso, are you alright?"

"My ankle hurts," she said, wincing. She felt her cheeks flush with anger as the words left her mouth.

Benitez turned to the man in the hat and shook his head.

The man pursed his lips and nodded, the look of disappointment painted on his face. He tipped his hat and walked away.

"Who was that man, Coach?"

He lifted her arm over his neck and helped her walk off the track. "That was a member of the International Olympic Committee."

She felt her heart sink into her chest. "Why was he here?"

"Calypso, I have something to tell you. But here, sit first." He guided her toward the grass, setting her down gently. "I don't know how to put this, but two weeks ago there was a major earthquake in the Pacific Ocean. A catastrophically large tsunami formed over Japan, wiping away most of the country."

"What do you mean?"

"Most of country, the islands... gone. Submerged. I'm afraid Japan no longer exists as it once did. I'm sorry, Calypso."

She lowered her head. Calypso knew she was supposed to feel grief, sadness, misery, but nothing came. How could it? The memory of her parents might as well have been an illusion, some half-remembered dream. Her knowledge of their homeland was even scarcer.

"Why was he here?" she repeated.

"The Olympic Committee has voted to allow Japan to participate in this summer's games, but as most of the athletes were killed, that proved a difficult task. They're scouting the world for Japanese descendants and athletes willing to form a new Japanese Olympic team. He was here to scout you. But this injury looks bad. I'm sorry."

The tears welled in her eyes. They trickled warmly down her cheeks. Coach Benitez hugged her. But she wasn't sad for a country she didn't know. In Lima, the means to survive and prosper were far and in between. Especially for someone like her. Around every corner in the city someone had been waiting to tease the way she looked, joke about foods she'd never eaten, or mock a language which was nothing but alien to her. No, the loss of Japan wasn't a concern to her. It was her future that was in question. For all she knew, her career as a runner was over before it even began.

"I'm so sorry, Calypso. I know what you must be going through. All we can do is pray to God and hope that his light can guide us in these times."

Calypso didn't know how to respond. She didn't pray to the Christian God. Nor the gods of the Incas, or whichever Shinto gods were revered in Japan. She'd known nothing of prayer or angels or spirits. The only religion she could invoke were the words she'd whispered to herself before every sprint as she tried in vain to calm her nerves.

She inhaled a deep breath and peered over to the bleachers again. The crowd sat and stared back. Why were they there? There weren't any sanctioned races, and it didn't seem like they were there to cheer anybody on. She wasn't sure if it had been the tears in her eyes distorting her vision, but the people in the stands appeared wispy and transparent, like ghosts.

"Who are those people there, Coach?"

He turned around. "There's nobody up there," he shrugged. "Look, you're tired. Go home and rest your ankle," Coach Benitez said, letting go. "This year's senior tryouts start next month. With any luck you'll be healed and ready to go."

After she'd procured her book bags from her locker, she limped towards the bus stop at the end of the street. The daily traffic of old jalopies and motorbikes buzzed by as stacks of grey smoke shot out of their exhaust pipes and spiraled up into Lima's sky.

Suddenly she heard a cacophony of footsteps tap down the street. She turned. The crowd from the bleachers approached and stopped alongside her besides the bus stop bench. Now she could see them clearly. There was no stench permeating from their bodies, but she could tell by the rot of their flesh that they were dead.

There must have been about fifty of them, all huddled together like a group of nervous tourists. Their faces were gaunt, some with eyes sunken through their sockets. Their bodies appeared semi-translucent, and they wore a medley of clothing styles ranging from modern to antiquated. Teenagers wore torn rock band shirts with faded Converse shoes. Some men wore suits with fedoras, while some of the women sported billowing kimonos. There were children wearing old school uniforms, and even a few scowling men wearing padded leather samurai armor.

She knew then that they were Japanese. Many of them had slim, angular faces like her, and all of them had the same slanted eyes she'd had. *Almond eyes*, the people in town used to tell her. Others had used less polite terms: *ojos Chinos*. Chinese eyes.

The group regarded her curiously, like patrons meticulously shopping for a puppy behind a wall of glass. The children seemed to be taken in by the sight of old cars or the balloon vendors on the corners.

"H-hello, my name is Calypso," she said, scanning their faces, not knowing who to address.

No one replied. They just stood in silence, watching her, judging her.

A shiver ran down the length of her spine and the hairs on her arms went prickly.

The bus arrived and creaked to a stop, swinging its doors open. Calypso boarded and picked a seat toward the back. The ghosts boarded along with her, shuffling past a few standing riders, the look of shock on their faces as the bus filled beyond capacity.

"Hey," the bus driver called out to Calypso. "Are they with you?"

"I don't think so. I don't know who they are."

"Well, they better pay their fare."

Calypso regarded the group of disheveled bodies, all in varying stages of decay. Then she noticed their feet had been hovering a few inches off the ground. "I don't think they have money. They're dead."

"Oh," the bus driver said. "Well, tell them this is the last time they do this. I don't do charity, especially for dead people."

"I don't speak their language," she said.

The bus driver scowled and jerked the clutch.

The doors hissed shut, and they proceeded to roll down the cracked and congested streets of Lima for an hour until it came upon the dirt roads on the outskirts of the city. The bus rattled and wobbled as it turned and twisted up the hilly pass that led to her neighborhood.

Some ghosts sat beside her, while the rest stood clutching the support straps in silence, swaying as the bus swayed. She was surprised she hadn't been afraid, but realized they hadn't done anything to cause alarm. She wanted to ask why they were following her, but she knew she wouldn't get an answer. All she could hope for was that maybe they'd dissipate into thin air as the day progressed.

Once the bus came out on the other end of the hill, Calypso looked upon the town with equal amounts of awe and sadness. San Cristobal. The slums sat nestled amongst the mountains surrounding the city, hidden behind a thick, oppressive fog. The sprawl of battered homes dotted the landscape, all painted in a slew of vibrant colors. Pink, orange, red, all festive and full of joy. The colors stood in stark contrast to the condition of their foundations. Many of the homes had been erected from moldy wood, cracked concrete, or rusted sheet metal.

Directly behind the squalor of the town and etched into the San Cristobal Mountain was a series of ascending stone steps that reached all 409 meters to the top. At the crown of the mountain stood a tall cross that overlooked all of San Cristobal and could even be seen from Lima. The cross was a symbol to the people below; a testament to those who were brave enough to cling to the faith of their fathers, a sign that their God had not yet abandoned them. Calypso had no such signs here.

The bus stopped at the mouth of town, where the businesses sold sodas and snacks to tourists that had wandered too far from Lima.

She took a painful step off the bus and limped toward her house, which sat all the way toward the foot of the mountain.

Even now she could smell the scents of the afternoon's lunch as the vendors cooked the papas rellenas, the choclo, and the humitas. Her stomach rumbled in the worst way. She'd only had enough money for the bus. To trade it in for breakfast at school meant a five-hour walk back home.

As she made her way forward, onlookers gasped and shrieked as they stuck their heads out of their shops.

"Fantasmas," the people whispered. "La niña esta embrujada." Ghosts. The girl is cursed.

Calypso turned. The ghosts were already tailing her. They kept their distance as they meandered behind, some of them slogging along with jaws agape as they ogled the town in wonder.

"Go and take your people with you," a woman shouted, dismissively waving a spatula in anger. "You'll bring ruin to our town like President Fujimori did. You'll bleed us dry. Do you understand what I'm saying to you?"

It was nothing new. Taunts, name-calling. They'd always reminded her she was a second-class citizen in this country. She'd never been Peruvian enough for them, and knew nothing about being Japanese. She had been stuck in some identity limbo since birth.

The only thing that meant anything to her was running track. It was in those moments when her feet pounded the floor and her arms swung ferociously that she truly felt joy. All that mattered was the race and the wind in her hair, where she was stuck in some timeless loop of everlasting bliss. Where nothing bad ever existed or mattered.

She turned away from the townsfolk and limped on. Life, it seemed, had indeed struck her with a series of curses. Since her parents' death, life in the slums was all she had known. Her father's friend Reynaldo Villca took her into his family and gifted her a job in his business collecting and sorting recyclable goods to be sold as scrap in Lima.

"Niña linda," a soft, muffled voice said.

Calypso looked around. A red Culpeo fox darted out from a bush.

"Hello," the fox said with a grin.

"Oh," Calypso said. "Hello."

"I come bearing sad tidings," the fox said.

"What would that be?" Calypso said, raising an eyebrow.

The fox turned to the horde of ghosts skulking about. "Oh, maybe I'm a little late. Perhaps you know?"

"About Japan?"

"Yes. I see. Well, that makes it easier on me."

"Who are you? I've never met a talking fox before."

"Not many have. I am a kami."

"Oh, I don't know what that is," Calypso said.

The fox galloped alongside her. "A kami is many things. We are spirits or ghosts, or guardians of nature and gods. I am your guardian kami. Your 'guardian angel,' so to speak."

As Calypso walked ahead, the terrain began to slope upward, causing more stress on her ankle.

"What is your name?" Calypso said, grunting with each step.

"I don't think I have one," the fox said, stopping to lick his paws. "Give me one."

"I don't think I can do that. Reynaldo won't even let me keep any of the stray dogs in town as pets, and to name something is to certify its worth. I'm afraid I can't keep you."

"I'm not your pet, Calypso, I'm your guardian."

"Okay. I'll call you *Zorro*."

"Ah. Zorro. It feels nice to have a name. Well, Calypso, I'm here to steer you onto the right course at this time of uncertainty."

"What do you mean?"

"Well, now that Japan is gone, I think it's time you understand your place in the world."

"My place?"

"We all have a place in the world."

"Oh, is that right? What's mine?"

"That's for you to decide."

"I don't understand."

"That is why I am here."

"Look," she said, shaking her head. "I'm heading home. You think you can unsummon all these ghosts away? My family wouldn't like them here."

"I can't unsummon away your past," Zorro said, brushing his tale along her leg. "No matter where you go, whenever you turn around, the past will always be there to wave back. Besides, they have nowhere else to go now."

"Those people are not my past. I don't even know them."

"May I introduce you to a few of them?"

Calypso stopped halfway to her house, where the buildings began to gradually crumble at their foundations. A woman stepped outside of her home, rocking a baby in her arms. She looked upon the spectral congregation with frightened curiosity, made the sign of the cross, and stepped back inside.

Zorro approached one of the men padded in thick leather armor. "This is Toyotomi Hideyoshi. He was a simple peasant that became a samurai and eventually a great military general. He united much of Japan and abolished slavery." Hideyoshi clutched the scabbard at his side and bowed at Calypso.

Calypso bit her lip, unsure of what to do. She awkwardly bowed back.

"And this," Zorro said pawing the leg of a bearded man in ancient ceremonial garb, "is Jimmu, the first emperor of Japan." The man raised his longbow and bowed his head.

"Oh, wow," she said, bowing even lower than before.

"Meet Kiichiro Toyoda, the founder of the world's largest automobile company, Toyota." A middle-aged man in glasses and a kind smile reached out to shake her hand. To her surprise, she shook a firm, warm hand.

A woman in a purple, flowing kimono bent over to pick up Zorro and cradled him against her chest. "Calypso, I'd like you to meet Murasaki Shikibu. She wrote the world's first novel, *The Tale of Genji*."

Calypso's face flushed as she again bowed. "Oh, my goodness. It is an honor to meet you. All of you. I didn't know any of this. I never had anyone to teach me these things. You are all such interesting people," she said. "But why are you telling me this, Zorro?" she asked, as she began to walk up the slope again.

"These achievements don't end on an island, Calypso," Zorro explained, trotting beside her. "They are a part of you whether you see it or not."

"I still don't understand."

"These memories, these legacies, these histories, they need a home. Without a connection, their spirits wither into the forgotten void. And a person without knowledge of their past is doomed to linger in an unhappy future."

As they came upon Calypso's house by the foot of the mountain, the group had already drawn a large crowd at their tail.

Many of the children picked up small stones and hurled them at the ghosts, yelling "Diablos orientales!" They ran back to hide behind the safety of their parents. The ghosts huddled closer together, ignoring the sharp taunts as the stones phased through their ethereal bodies.

Reynaldo had been painting the house in a fresh coat of red paint while his wife Mireya hung some sheets to dry on a clothesline when they noticed the ruckus.

"Calypso, what is going on?"

"I don't know," she said, hobbling toward the house. "They just followed me home. I'm going to get some rest. I sprained my ankle on the track today."

"No, you're going to help us paint the house before the sun goes down."

"But I can barely walk."

Reynaldo's brows furrowed as he pointed the paintbrush at Calypso. "You're going to help this family and start pulling your weight around here. No more sob stories about losing your parents, no more blowing off your responsibilities because you want to go run a race somewhere. When you graduate, you're coming straight to the family business. You and your people there," he waved at the crowd of ghosts, "have been leeching off us real Peruvians for far too long, leaving us to do the heavy work while they line their pockets."

Calypso felt the sting in her heart. She had known that Japanese roots had gone far and deep in Peru. They had settled as farmers and business owners and had been loyal patriots for some time. While it was true that some Japanese descendants had in the past run a corrupt government in Peru, she'd had nothing to do with that. Their names were just as foreign to her as the Quechua elders of history. She turned to face the ghosts. Her head throbbed and her brows furrowed.

"Why are they judging me for things I haven't done?" She jabbed a finger in the direction of the specters. "And how can people see these ghosts, anyway?"

"Because," Zorro said, "no matter where you live, what you do, or how noble you may act, people will always see you and the faces of your ancestors in the distance, trailing like a shadow. And those who are especially critical will damn you for their missteps for as long as you live. You must find yourself and accept the past with an eye to the future. Past and present must reconcile. You must find yourself so that both may be at peace."

"What do you mean? How do I do this?" she asked, tears streaming down her eyes.

"You really are cursed, Calypso," Reynaldo said. "Now a talking fox?"

The fox nuzzled her leg. "Accept who you are and those who came before, because no one else will do that for you. In Shinto, it is customary to pay respect to those departed with a shrine or an act of goodwill."

"Calypso," Reynaldo said. "Do you hear me?"

"My whole life," she said, "I've lived with the guilt and shame of my lineage. And I never knew why. I never had heroes to look up to. I've lived trying to appease others without creating an identity for myself." She turned toward Reynaldo. "My name is Aiko. Aiko Calypso Tanaka." She snatched Reynaldo's paintbrush and yanked a white sheet off the clothesline.

"What are you doing?" Mireya shouted.

Calypso painted a large red circle on the sheet and jogged toward the steps of Cerro San Cristobal, the small mountain beyond her house.

Zorro and the ghosts followed her.

As she climbed the steps, her ankle stiffened, shooting burning jolts through her nerves. She clenched her teeth and shook her head, trying to ignore the pain.

Once she reached the halfway point, the fog became denser and the air colder. She turned. The line of spirits stretched down like a row of dominoes behind her. In that line ran the spectrum of Japan's heritage all the way from the beginning. Heroes and villains, nobles and peasants, city folk and farmers.

In the distance among the hovels and the dirt, she could see the townspeople flailing their arms about like angry little ants.

There was a fire in her lungs now as she gasped as her feet pushed off every step of stone.

The wind lashed and pulled at her clothing. Her legs kicked and pushed off with the force of an Olympic sprinter.

As she reached the crown of the mountain she stepped past the cross and onto the edge where she looked upon the sprawling vista, where Lima stretched into the Pacific Ocean. Calypso raised her arms. The flag flapped ferociously in the cool Peruvian air.

The ghosts were already alongside her, smiling and bowing at the sight of their future. They had found a home.

"Zorro," she said. "I hope those people down there won't be too mad."

The fox paused to survey the city below. "Flags," he said, "have been waved for conquest, pride, and supremacy. But there is no reason more noble than to claim 'I am here. I live. I belong.' And that is all."

Aiko Calypso Tanaka smiled as she waved the Japanese flag. Just then, the pain in her ankle rescinded. And out there among the people, her people, the future began to look as bright as a rising sun.

The Gentle War

"Keep your voice down, Maya," Anderson James whispered, "we don't want them to hear us." He lowered his head and removed his lab badge, shoving it in his back pocket.

Maya Mercado raised an eyebrow. She saw no reason for secrecy. Their avian overlords weren't exactly known to round people up and torture them for gossiping. Besides their draconian peacetime policies, the Nuumbies were very docile creatures; angelic looking, even. Either way, she thought, the downtown streets were unusually busy for a Tuesday night and the buzz of chatter had drowned out their conversation. Still, Anderson was always one for caution.

"So you're saying," Maya said doing her best to keep her voice low, "that the Mothership above Earth's orbit has no weapons?"

Anderson looked around, surveying the streets as if the information he harbored would be grounds for extreme punishment. A few Nuumbie sentries patrolled the boulevard, craning their long necks every which way, making sure any drunken provocations followed the *Gentle Treaty.* "That's what our readouts tell us," he said at last. "We found no signs of warheads, or laser cannons, or anything remotely resembling projectile-based weapons. Besides the ship's drive, there are no signs of considerable energy readouts, either. It's just that massive ship and the AI that runs it."

"Interesting," she said looking up at the night sky, hoping to glimpse a look at the ship hovering in orbit. No luck. She remembered seeing it a few times during her life, that giant pyramid-shaped object just hovering in the sky like a raft on a tranquil lake. "What about that big EMP that wiped out all of Earth's weapons a while back?"

"We're still not sure how they pulled it off, but I can tell you they don't have anything resembling conventional weapons of mass destruction."

"So we just gave in to their demands and they weren't even armed?" Maya giggled. "So no weapons. What do you think it means?"

Before Anderson could answer, someone bumped into her shoulder. Maya's body spun from the force of the blow, nearly toppling her to the ground.

A man in a hockey jersey who smelled of cheap, potent vodka turned to her. "Watch where the hell you're going, broad!"

"Screw you," she said, squaring up with the man and shoving him with both hands.

The man drew a switchblade from his waist and flung the knife open. "I'm gonna kill you," the man said, slurring his words.

Maya shifted into a defensive posture and prepared for the man's lunge.

As the drunkard cocked his hand back an alarm blared out across the street. Sirens embedded on lampposts flashed angrily, casting the long, gnarled shadows of hundreds of civilians on the streets. "Halt," a voice shouted behind them.

A Nuumbie sentry stepped between them, shooting its white, plumed wings outward. A smattering of feathers danced on the night's breeze like falling leaves. It stood roughly six feet tall, with a lean, delicate body, and moved with the grace of an intergalactic ballerina. The Nuumbie held a webbed hand up. "Physical acts of violence are outlawed. All threats of violence are to be carried out in accordance with the Gentle Treaty. I will distribute the appropriate weapons to the combatants and allow the dispute to be resolved in the proper manner. Whoever becomes Marked first will be beamed directly to the Mothership and face the consequences. Do the parties wish to continue?"

A crowd started to gather, most of them curious as to the process that was about to unravel before them. In the thirty years since Nuumbie rule, very few cases of *Gentle* conflicts had taken place. All of Earth had bowed to Nuumbie Law from fear of the consequences.

Maya looked at the drunkard. Beads of sweat started to collect on his forehead. His eyebrows came together in frustration. He eyed Maya in contempt before stepping back. "No. We're fine here," he said. "It's the playoffs and she's not worth it."

"Yeah," Maya said turning to the sentry. "There's no quarrel here."

"Very well," said the Nuumbie, bowing his head. "Move along."

As the man stumbled away, Anderson placed a hand on Maya's shoulder. "Are you alright?"

"Yeah, I'm fine," she sighed. "I could've taken that guy."

"How do you know? You've never fought anyone in your life."

"I doubt he has either," she said.

Once they made their way to O'Malley's Bar they settled into their usual booth by the back corner. It was Anderson's favorite spot, away from the prying eyes of nosy drunkards and curious Nuumbies. Emily, their waitress, blew a tuft of hair from her face and slammed down two perspiring mugs of beer. She smiled at Anderson and padded off toward the bar.

Anderson ran a trembling hand through his hair. He had been acting his usual anxious self, and Maya had offered to buy her best friend some drinks if he'd agree to come out for once. Anderson knew if you followed their rules there was nothing to fear, but he liked to play it safe and stay home after work anyway.

Maya took a swig from her beer as Anderson slumped over his drink, looking like he'd rather be at home taking care of his mother. She didn't blame him; a dementia patient was nothing to gloss over.

"We have to show them we're not afraid," she said at last, placing a soft hand on his. "We have to live our lives. Screw 'em."

"I don't intend to question them. I'm afraid of what might happen," he said, looking down at his amber-colored reflection in the mug.

"No one knows what happens."

"Exactly my point. No one's ever come back. And you know I can't leave Mom alone. She wouldn't make it without me."

The question regarding the *Marked* had gnawed away at her brain her whole life, and she knew it was best not to ponder, but she asked him anyway. "What do you think happens to the Marked?"

"I don't want to know."

"Sure you do. You know what I think? I think everyone who's whisked away endures a life of slave labor in the service of that AI master of theirs."

"Or used as nourishment for the Nuumbies. Maybe they put a halt to our violence so they have more sustenance available." Anderson's eyes welled. He'd been frightened like the same boy she'd known in grade school. Maya took another sip of beer and regretted starting the conversation. Anderson's mood had soured. She tried desperately to think of something to distract him.

"So how does their tech work? I mean the weapons they dispense for the *Gentle* conflicts?"

"Well, we've never gotten our hands on one, but there has been some speculation over at the lab." Anderson finally took a sip of his beer. He straightened in his seat. The subject seemed to stir him to life. "The Gentle Treaty, as you know, is the Nuumbie law meant to discourage violence and murder by replicating the process in a non-violent confrontation. The results are meant to emulate the impact of lost lives by permanently removing the Marked from Earth. No one dies, but they leave our world forever. Their form of settling disputes harmlessly with all of the heavy consequences and none of the mess. Their way of teaching us a lesson, I suppose. Like an angry intergalactic parent. Like angels from above."

"I've never actually seen it happen," she said, curious and afraid at the same time.

"It's like a legally sanctioned duel. Since they banned all of Earth's firearms and weapons, they dispense pistols very similar to our paintball guns. The ammunition works the same way. The projectile ball breaks on the opponent's body, thereby Marking them. The marking is representative of realdeath and the *dead* are immediately beamed to the Mothership, never to be seen again."

"That's heavy. How do the paintballs work?"

"We don't know, but if you ask me, I think there has to be some sort of radioactive material in the paint. The AI Mothership then locks on to the unique energy source and beams up anyone that's been tagged, dispensing its brand of justice to them indiscriminately." He inhaled a large gulp of beer. "In regards to your question about why the Mothership doesn't have any weapons..." He paused and looked around again. "I think we're dealing with some ancient AI. When I look at the Nuumbies, I think *there's no way they created that ship in orbit.* Their aesthetics don't match, and the Nuumbies clearly don't appear as a warring race or as martial colonizers. Maybe it was a policing program that ran amok and now it travels the stars, looking to subject any living beings it finds to its creator's laws. Maybe the Nuumbies were just like us at one point until the Mothership found them and scared them into complying with its mission. Perhaps the creators of the thing met some cruel fate, too, and they were done in by their own creation."

"That's terrifying," she said, shaking her head. "Call me crazy, but I've always been one to believe that conflict leads to progress if we're smart enough to learn from it. I mean, think about it; without war we'd never have high-powered rockets, and no rockets means we never would've started a space program, and so forth. I think they should leave us to our own devices and let us figure it all out. We don't need space nannies telling us how to live our lives."

"I mean, I know I'm sounding hypocritical but what if they're right, though? What if we as a species can't be trusted to our own devices?"

"Then what's the point of living?"

A loud murmur erupted in the bar as the patrons sprang from their seats and rushed toward the television sets by the counter. "Turn up the volume," someone yelled.

A news anchor stiffened in his seat and stared glumly at the camera. "The development comes as a shock as both countries had been on the verge of meaningful negotiations. But now to confirm: talks between China and the United States have broken down and both nations have formally agreed to war in keeping with the Gentle Treaty in order to resolve their longstanding dispute."

The crowd let out a collective gasp proceeded by silence. Mouths hung agape in collective sadness and the only sound was of glass shattering on the floor.

The anchor continued: "Now the random process of Selective Service will be instituted in accordance with the Treaty. Folks, tell your loved ones how much they mean to you. It may very well be the last time you see them."

Maya's phone rumbled. An unlisted number. She swiped her phone and stared at the screen. A message from the U.S. Government. She set the phone on the counter, the message unread. She knew, though, and her heart sank into her bowels.

Soon Anderson's phone rumbled, too.

Then the rumbling rang across the bar and even outside as people paused in the middle of the street, gawking dumbly at their phones.

Maya turned to look at Anderson. His tears were already dripping into his beer.

⁓

It was her turn to jump. She adjusted the goggles on her face and swallowed a hard lump of nothing. Her throat was dry and scratchy, and she wanted a beer in the worst way to settle her nerves. She crouched and jumped from the dropship.

The fall wasn't a long one, and she landed in an ankle-deep pool of water on a rice paddy that helped cushion her fall.

All around her lay green, wet fields and hilly terrain covering the horizon. The sun was bright and if it weren't for her goggles, she'd be blinded by now. Up ahead, a dense grouping of red uniforms gathered across the way, waiting for their arrival.

The rest of the troops dropped in behind her as the enemy line opened fire on their position. A few stray rounds tagged some of the solders mid-fall, the purple paint splashing over their torsos like blood. They screamed in terror as their bodies dissolved in a particle stream before they even hit the mud.

A flash of a shadow painted the field as a Nuumbie darted overhead. It soared above the conflict in slow, lazy circles like a bird of prey biding its time. Maya eyed the outskirts of the battlefield. On the sidelines stood a number of Nuumbie referees, their necks jerking about as they witnessed the horror. Their job, she was briefed, was to ensure that nobody tried to sneak out of the conflict or cheated by slipping real guns into the equation. Those who did would be punished the same as the rest: they'd be Marked and beamed away forever. Angels from Heaven.

Up ahead thousands of Chinese troops advanced swiftly, trying to take advantage of the lag in U.S. troop deployment. A number of enemy soldiers knelt down and unleashed a torrent of heavy suppressing fire, pinning the recently deployed like fish in a barrel. About twenty of her companions got hit, their bodies flailing like palm trees in a storm.

The violent whooshing sounds of wind startled her while the paintballs whizzed beside her face. She dropped her head and rushed forward, trying not to think about Anderson. Maya hadn't seen him since basic training. She hoped that wherever he was, he was taking cover somewhere safe. "Hang in there, Anderson," she said under her breath. "Your mom needs you."

A woman Maya recognized from O'Malley's crouched beside her. Emily. Yes, Emily! It was a slight comfort to lay eyes upon someone familiar. So many strangers fighting beside her and not a one to offer words of comfort.

"Hey," the woman said, recognizing her as well. She placed a soft hand on Maya's shoulder and offered a gentle shake. "Good luck out there, Sis. We gotta win this one. I got kids waiting for me back home. They need their-"

Wack!

A ball splattered on Emily's goggles. She shrieked and clawed at her face, trying in vain to wipe the paint away. In another moment her body dissolved in a flash of light. Maya dropped to the ground and belly crawled forward. Her lips quivered while she held back the tears she wanted so badly to weep.

Above, dropships unloaded their last passengers and banked away sharply from the hot zone. The sound of screams and wind ripping overhead intensified while the battle reached its apex.

She raised her gun slightly above her face and took a few blind, arching potshots, hoping to clear some kind of room ahead of the wet ditch she was pinned down to.

A group of roughly thirty U.S. troops approached her position and advanced as they laid down a hail of fire.

Maya knew big pockets of soldiers like that drew the most attention, like a big, fleshy target. Soon, her position would be inundated with falling paintballs. She rolled to her side and climbed out of the paddy just as a heavy grouping of balls rained down on her team. She ignored their screams as best she could while she clawed out of the ditch.

About a dozen yards away, a Nuumbie referee watched from the sidelines of the battlefield, its gun slung behind its shoulder. Its features were mostly avian: a pair of eyes, wings, webbed hands and feet, a beak now curling slightly upward in what appeared to be a smile. It scanned the field, nodding in approval with every splattered ball. The Nuumbie appeared to be taking joy in the event. She'd never seen one of them smile before.

Maya spared a glimpse at the battle. Chinese and American troops— men and women alike— screamed across the field. Beams of light sparkled madly across the hills as thousands of troops left Earth every second. She felt her face warm as the blood rushed through her body. Just then, anger replaced the fear she'd felt, and she knew hate. Not for the strangers across the way but for the invaders who'd planted their flag on her world and told her how to live. A gust of wind rippled across the grass, and she let its cool breeze soothe her. Suddenly, she noticed her hand had been raised at eye level, stretched out beyond her body. She'd already been staring down the sights of her gun. A slew of balls whipped past her as she took a few steps forward.

She focused down the sights. The Nuumbie's head squared up perfectly down the barrel. The alien noticed. It frowned and slung its weapon around. She squeezed the trigger.

Bang!

She squeezed again.

Bang!

And again.

And again.

Splat.

The ball broke on its face, smearing it with purple goop. The Nuumbie fell to its knees, raised its arms to the sky as if to plead for mercy, and screeched madly. A violent flash of light enveloped the alien's body before its molecules split apart and dissolved completely.

The battlefield fell silent.

It didn't take longer than a few seconds for both armies to catch on. American and Chinese troops turned toward the Nuumbies with vigor.

And the paintballs filled the air. Nuumbies were shot out of the sky, blasted on the ground, all dissolving in a manic show of light. Nuumbie bodies flashed out of existence until none were left on the field.

They'd feared the same weapons they'd administered to humans. The punishment aboard the Mothership must have been something to dread. Whatever awaited them was a nightmare of untold terrors.

Maya smiled.

She knew, then, what was coming. A unified front. History in the making. Mankind had found a mutual objective and a common enemy. Learning from conflict. In a way, she had peered into the future. Humanity now had the enemy's weapons at their disposal, perhaps even to reverse engineer. Soon, in time, even the Mothership would be in their sights.

And she felt pride, joy, and even the slightest bit of pity for the Nuumbies. Because she knew, with these weapons in their hands and the ones to come after, they wouldn't be afforded a gentle war.

The *S*andbox

Deacon squinted, looking past the sand dunes. He'd seen the ocean before, but never one of endless sand. The heat rose in the distance, mangling the air into contorted waves.

Just over the horizon of endless dust lay the border. They'd never been this far before, and he couldn't help but feel nervous. He kept his revolver in one hand and a battered teddy bear in the other. One could never be too sure what was out there.

In the sky, broken remnants of ancient starships hung in orbit just under the glaring sun. Vestiges of their battle with the space invaders the previous week. Behind him, the squeak of rusted wheels approached.

Hidalgo pulled up beside him, hauling the dilapidated red wagon.

"What's beyond the border?" Deacon said, his voice cracking. The last word sounded shrill, like when you squeezed an old dog toy in your hand. He was surprised the noise came out of him and he hoped Hidalgo hadn't noticed.

"That's the end of the Sandbox, amigo," Hidalgo said, seemingly ignoring Deacon's gaffe. He nodded to himself in awe while gazing at the desert. "Looks like we've made it to the end."

"What do you think is out there? Bandits? Robots? More monsters?"

"I don't really know, Deak. I heard it's something worse. Much worse."

"Worse?" Deacon asked, stroking the newfound hairs on his chin. He didn't remember those being there last week. He couldn't wait to get home and stand in front of his mirror to get a look. It had been a while since he'd been home. He couldn't even remember how long it'd been since the last sight of Momma or one of her beef stews steaming in the pot.

"Mmhm. They say the Elders live there. People say they have the answers to all of life's riddles. All we have to do is go over there and show them our respects."

"You don't say," Deacon said.

"Yes, sir. Always have to respect the Elders. Also heard the wickedest thug in the West lives there. The one they call Responsa Billy."

Deacon squeezed the teddy bear against his torso. The gash in the bear's side spat out a clump of cotton entrails. All three of them had been through a lot of action, but Deacon wasn't sure how much longer the game would last. Soon, summer would be coming to a close. After that, the future seemed cloudy. "I don't wanna deal with no Responsa Billy."

"I'm afraid we have to," Hidalgo said, taking a breath and tipping the rim of his hat. "We all gotta deal with Responsa Billy at some point. That's what my father used to say. Nowhere else to go but forward."

Deacon pursed his lips. Hidalgo was right. All these years trekking through the Sandbox had gotten stale. They'd already done it all: they had discovered all the treasures there were to find; hunted down every boogeyman that roamed the highways; giggled at every dirty joke they'd heard. All that was left was the world beyond the box. And it scared them both. But they had each other and they'd never let the other one down.

Deacon propped the teddy bear on the wagon and snapped open his pistol's cylinder. Counting with the fingers on his hand, he noted how many caps remained inside the plastic chambers. "Four," he whispered to himself, and nodded. "Okay, let's do this," he said.

Hidalgo smiled and hoisted the red wagon's handle. Together, smiling, they crossed the border into the unknown.

The Final Gift

The sky was the color of twilight, and the ground was the color of rust. The three of them hunkered over spilled power tools as they repaired the damaged axle on the ATV. That's when Sergei Avilov tugged on Captain Julius Roeper's arm and pointed to the pale blue twinkle of light in the sky. As he hoisted a new tire into the chassis of the ATV, he looked up. When he saw it, Roeper tapped Rahmani's shoulder. The Iranian turned and wiped the red soil from his visor. They gazed upwards in silence. The dot in the sky twinkled as specks of orange light pulsed sporadically between pulses of blue light.

For hours, Earth flickered like a candle. As their oxygen ran low, they fired up the ATV and departed for the dome.

They slumped forward with their elbows on the table. They'd waited by the radio for hours.

Sergei pinched the knob on the receiver, turning it every few seconds to the sound of white noise. Sometimes brief static crackled. Mostly there was nothing.

Rahmani tapped his fingers on the table mindlessly, like a drunk man playing piano. Roeper rested his cheek on his fist, his gaze fixed on the wall.

Then there was a voice. The radio cut in and out, alternating between static and a ramble of staccato chatter:

"Nuclear strikes on all major cities." Crrrrk. "Heavy devastation. Fallout has contaminated the air." Crrrrk. "Cannot send for help."

The transmission died. A flatline beep. Then nothing.

The men looked at each other, then, each in his own contemplative way, looked at the floor. It was all the religion they could invoke. They held a moment of silence, grieving for all things lost.

After some hours, they gathered the courage to look each other in the eyes. The end. Curtains. Nail in the coffin for the human race.

The three of them on a cold, red rock and not a woman among them.

Roeper swung his fist across Rahmani's face. The Iranian dropped to his knees, his lips spewing vulgarities and red mist. Avilov tackled Roeper, slamming his shoulder into the captain's chest. As he toppled down, the back of his head connected to the steel plated floor.

Rahmani lunged at Avilov, grabbed the back of his collar, and heaved him into the wall.

Roeper stood and spat blood. The captain laughed and jabbed a finger at each man.

The three of them barked accusations, each blaming the other for Nuclear Armageddon. They squabbled over which country had the most bombs and who had the motives to use them. This happened until their mouths were dry and their throats raw.

Then, one by one, they sat at the table again, staring at the walls like punished children.

It was cold inside the dome. Especially in the months since the final transmission. Quiet and icy. Like death.

The air hummed from the vents like a distant generator, the hairs on Roeper's arms erect needles. He walked toward the airlock door and peered through the window. His breath fogged up the glass as he stared at the basin outside. The blowback from his breath greeted him, and he took comfort in its warmth. Warmth. He leaned into the window and blew forcefully into the glass. The condensation shrouded his view as droplets of moisture trickled down the pane. He flicked away the moisture and peered outside. The shuttle sat undisturbed in a coat of red dust a few kilometers from the dome.

He looked at the men, slouching in their chairs.

He smiled.

He had an idea.

———❧———

Roeper clicked 'stop' on the recorder and placed it on the table. The hard drive sat inside a safe box beside it. Inside its banks lay stored much of the knowledge accumulated through human history.

They exited the airlock. Outside, a breeze kicked up a red sandstorm. Three kilometers west, the *Genesis* jutted out like a fossil from the dirt, the shuttle that brought them to Mars so many months before. The main thrusters were lost, but its nuclear-powered engines enabled the craft to fly inside the Martian atmosphere.

The men mounted the ATV and looked at each other; their reflections stared back. The vehicle rumbled like a mechanical bull as it rolled over rocky terrain. Nothing was said along the way as each man stared off into the horizon.

When they arrived, it stood as a behemoth against the lonely landscape.

They boarded the hull, secured themselves, and reactivated the power.

An exhaust of blue fire shot out the underbelly of the ship, kicking up a blizzard of dirt. The *Genesis* lifted off the ground until it hovered above the Martian plain and thrust southward.

The shuttle flew over vast plains pockmarked with craters, dormant volcanoes keeping watch over chasms like sentries. Rahmani removed his helmet, resting his forehead against a port window. Avilov relinquished his hands from the controls and switched to autopilot. He walked beside Rahmani and peered outside. Roeper watched them as they stared wide-eyed in awe.

The Red Planet.

Roeper approached another window and gazed below. For a moment, the three of them watched together.

———❧———

The land ahead became a mass of icy swirls, akin to giant white thumbprints. The southern ice caps reminded Roeper of the ones on Earth, where they'd trained for years.

Avilov hunched over the screen, toying with the calibrations. The screen pinged. Roeper leaned over Avilov's shoulder, glimpsing a view at the monitor. The shuttle's ground-penetrating radar located its objective, located on a large ice sheet a few kilometers from the South Pole.

Rahmani looked at Roeper. The captain gave him a thumbs-up, and the crewmember keyed the coordinates into the system.

The shuttle lurched as it adjusted course.

Roeper thought about the mission. The three of them tasked with terraforming Mars. That was moot now. But just for now.

He'd remembered something else. Years before the mission, scientists uncovered a considerable deposit of carbon dioxide buried near the southern pole. They'd posited that if the ice sheets melted, the carbon dioxide would release into the atmosphere, creating a greenhouse effect, warming the surface of the planet, resulting in an expanded surface area where water could persist without boiling or refreezing. The foundation for a sustainable, living planet.

A release that large required extreme levels of energy. The kind stored in the engines of the *Genesis*.

Roeper walked toward the command console and pulled the throttle. He returned to his seat and secured his harness. Rahmani and Avilov followed suit.

The ship increased speed. The chairs groaned as the welds began to crack. Terminal velocity. Their insides twisted in freefall as the ship descended toward the ice cap.

They looked at each other a final time. Outside the cockpit window, the ice sheets grew large until all they saw was white. Roeper smiled. He thought it looked beautiful.

⁓

Audio Log of Captain Julius Roeper:

This is Captain Julius Roeper of the Martian Exploration Unit. My crew consists of co-pilot and geologist Sergei Avilov, and our engineer Arad Rahmani. We were tasked with establishing a small, sustainable colony on Mars.

Four months ago, we witnessed what we believe to be the destruction of our home planet, Earth. We received a final transmission stating that our world had succumbed to a nuclear war. We've heard nothing since.

We don't know what happened, and that's the hardest thing. I suppose we won't ever know.

Whether it was the hatred we carried towards one another or the quest for power, it doesn't matter in the end.

All I can do is pray that not everyone on Earth is dead. If that's true, humanity will endure. The pieces will be put back together. But I know that may be a long time from now. You, like us, are now stranded on a desolate rock, far from help. And if you decide to come back here, well, we'll be long gone.

We cannot procreate. There were no women on this crew. But we three have decided to do something, and quite honestly, we don't know if it'll work. If it doesn't, we'll be dead, and that'll be that. But if it does, we would like to leave you with a final gift in the hopes that things will be different then.

You may never know how desolate and lifeless this planet was, but for the future generations of explorers, maybe hundreds or thousands of years from now, we would like to leave you with hope. The hope of clean water, a breathable atmosphere, rich soil, and the good intents that come only with brotherhood.

Much love, now and always.

Captain Julius Roeper and the crew of the MEU.

End Audio Log.

Story Notes

"Magic Lucha"— This is a fantasy story about family and the healing power of curandera magic. It's also about brujas, Mexico, abuelas, and lucha libre, which I grew up watching with my dad on TV. I enjoy utilizing Mexican culture in my stories as homage to my family and my roots. Growing up, the fantasy books and movies I was exposed to were very Eurocentric, but I'd like to see more diverse representation in the genre. Magic belongs to every culture and our words give it life.

"A Final Song for the Ages"— This story is about loneliness and being the last of your kind while stranded in a faraway world. It was inspired by the Kaua'i 'ō'ō, an extinct Hawaiian bird last spotted in 1985, and last recorded in 1987. The last recording of the bird captured a lone male's beautifully distinct mating song, intended for a female which would never respond. It ultimately lost its habitat to predators and habitat destruction. This inspired the fictional kipi—kua in my story, a blind, pangolin—like animal that is the last of its kind. This also informed the narrative around Nora, an orphan and the sole survivor of a doomed generation ship. Sometimes it's the little things that keep us going, like memories or the songs of our people, no matter how grim the circumstances.

"Echoes and Embers"— I wanted to combine horror and science—fiction to tell a unique ghost story set in the ruins of a post—apocalyptic Los Angeles. Particle accelerators, time travel, trauma. The resulting story addresses hauntings in a unique way.

"Sierra Starfall and the Elders of the Spaceways"— I'm a fan of Robert E. Howard, Star Wars, and Sword and Planet stories like *A Princess of Mars*, so this was my take on all those elements. Swashbuckling space pirates, an asteroid, psychedelic spores, crazed miners, and elder gods. This was a fun ride.

"Dracosaurus Reborn"— This was my first story sale back in 2009. A 100—word drabble about genetic engineering and reviving things that should have stayed dead. I still look back on this story and smile.

"Legacy"— An homage to books, libraries, Ray Bradbury, and classic SF. Set in a post—apocalyptic Mexico, where the last man on Earth barricades himself inside a library and makes a last stand against alien invaders set on destroying human knowledge and history. A statement on war, censorship, and book burning, something I think is very relevant these days.

"The Facsimile War"— This military SF story involves Felix, a Chicano convict from Earth who, in exchange for freedom, takes a plea deal to fight a war on a distant planet against an enemy he knows nothing about. His body is beamed six light—years away, a process which de—atomizes and rearranges his body, effectively killing him and creating him anew, albeit as an amnesiac with no sense of self or purpose. The war he has been contracted to fight has been raging for 100 years against a relentless vampiric enemy. Facing annihilation, Felix comes to learn some terrifying secrets about his new battlefield on planet Ruun. This story is a critique against forever wars, colonization, and the industrial prison complex, which tends to swallow people up, use them, and spit them out worse monsters than when they first went in.

"Do as I Do"— A story set in Mexico during the robot apocalypse, featuring a young woman teaching a domestic robot to become more human than even she thought possible. This is a story about finding oneself and returning to nature. About escaping the jaws of the machines and learning to become human all over again. It is also about life. One of my favorite stories.

"Sneeze"— A SF/magic realist hybrid about a grandfather teaching his grandson some very important secrets about the nature of the universe. I've often wondered if our own world is a universe—within—a—

universe; one of many, constantly birthing and dying in an endless loop.

"Portals to the Past"— A flash fiction piece featuring time travel, a father, and an endearing gift from another time. Sometimes love transcends time itself.

"The Seeds of Foundation"— This story about terraforming, funerals, and a son's love for his father is dedicated to immigrant fathers around the world who have had to traverse borders and foreign lands to achieve their dreams and create brighter futures for their children and the generations that follow. These acts of love sow the seeds of foundation for a better tomorrow.

"The Tailor of Worlds"— A two—man crew piloting a generation ship whose passengers are in cryostasis get pulled into a wormhole and experience a behind—the—curtains look at the mechanizations of the universe itself. I wanted to weave science—fiction with a secret mythology of the cosmos. Something that straddled the line between science—fiction and dreamlike fantasy.

"The Protean Tether"— *Neuromancer* meets *The Call of Cthulhu* in this Lovecraftian/cyberpunk story set in dystopian Nylax City. This was a fun story to write, as cyberpunk is one of my favorite SF subgenres and cosmic/weird fiction is one of my favorite horror subgenres. Slick, weird, horrifying, dreamlike, it has many elements I love about genre fiction.

"The Carnivorous Planet"— Another military SF story, this one with elements of eco—horror. This story exists in the same universe as "The Facsimile War," and shows us the plight of the populace of another generation ship as it finds itself colonizing a planet that may well be alive, angry, and not very receptive to destructive guests. Plant/human—zombie hybrids are just one of many problems facing the colonists on planet Jannah.

"Second Chances"— I took the premise of *What would happen if Tejano singer Selena Quintanilla Pérez had never been killed?* and *What would the world look like if that were the case?* Set in a near future Houston, where the oceans have risen, and an inquisitive high school student learns that actions lead to unintended ripples across multiple timelines.

"The Incident at Chicxulub"— I wanted to tackle the racist legacy of H.P. Lovecraft and counter it with the mythology of the Mexican people in what amounts to a cool kaiju showdown for the ages. Oftentimes, writing speculative fiction feels like playing in a giant sandbox and this is a great example.

"The Revolution Engine"— A Dieselpunk story set in the Mexican desert during the 1950s as a small band of refinery workers take on Soviet forces with advanced technology. A fun, David vs. Goliath alternate—history romp.

"Calypso and the Kami"— A story of ghosts, a kami, and a Japanese—Peruvian high school student struggling to come to terms with who she is amidst daily struggles with racism and a global catastrophe. I wanted to tackle the racism that lives in Latin America but is rarely spoken about with this story. Sometimes people from different cultural backgrounds find themselves ostracized, when in truth, these people have had roots in Latin America for generations.

"The Gentle War"— A military SF story with a not—so—violent twist. What if alien invaders found a solution to ending violent confrontations on Earth utilizing non—violent means? What if that solution also consisted of an imposed dictatorship? Would we accept their terms? Or fight back?

"The Sandbox"— Magic realism, science—fiction, allegory. After years of sharing many adventures, two soon—to—be—teenagers traverse the sandbox one last time to face their biggest challenge yet. This is an allegory for growing up. The awkward bridge from childhood to the start of adulthood, where our days of make—believe are in their twilight and the onset of responsibility arrives.

"The Final Gift"— As the nuclear apocalypse rages on Earth, three astronauts stranded on Mars must come to terms with their fate. Isolated, angry, and out of options, they have one last card to play that may shape the course of human history. A doomsday scenario with a sliver of hope, and hopefully, a lesson to humanity that with cooperation, we can achieve great things.

Publication History

"Magic Lucha," originally published in *Worlds of Possibility*, 2022.

"A Final Song for the Ages," originally published in *Infinite Constellations: An Anthology of Identity, Culture, and Speculative Conjunctions*, edited by Khadijah Queen & K. Ibura, FC2 (University of Alabama Press), 2023.

"Echoes and Embers," originally published in *The Place Where Everyone's Name is Fear*, edited by Cody Sexton & Sebastian Vice, Anxiety Press/Outcast Press, 2022.

"Sierra Starfall and the Elders of the Spaceways," originally published in *Planet Scumm #9*, 2020.

"Dracosaurus Reborn," originally published in *The Drabbler #14*, 2009.

"Legacy," is original to this collection.

"The Facsimile War," originally published in *El Porvenir ¡Ya! Citlalzazanilli Mexicatl, a Chicano Science Fiction Anthology*, edited by Scott Russell Duncan, Jenny Irizary, & Armando Rendon, Somos en Escrito Literary Foundation Press, 2022.

"Do as I Do," originally published in *Speculative Fiction for Dreamers*, edited by Alex Hernandez, Matthew David Goodwin, & Sarah Rafael Garcia, Mad Creek Books (Ohio State University Press), 2021.

"Sneeze," originally published in *Somos en Escrito Literary Magazine*, 2020.

"Portals to the Past," originally published in *Drabble Harvest #2*, 2014.

"The Seeds of Foundation," originally published in *Crossed Genres #19*, 2014.

"The Tailor of Worlds," is original to this collection.

"The Protean Tether," originally published in *The Scribe Magazine*, 2020.

"The Carnivorous Planet," originally published in *Full Metal Horror III: The Unknown*, edited by Sam M. Phillips & Adam Bennett, Zombie Pirate Publishing, 2020.

"Second Chances," is original to this collection.

"The Incident at Chicxulub," originally published in *The Were-Traveler*, 2020.

"The Revolution Engine," originally published in *Gaslandia: A Dieselpunk Anthology*, edited by Lesley Sabga & Elizabeth O. Smith, Radiant Crown Publishing, 2018.

"Calypso and the Kami," originally published in *The Scribe Magazine*, 2020.

"The Gentle War," is original to this collection.

"The Sandbox," originally published in *Unity Volume 1: A Magical Realism Anthology*, edited by Maria J. Estrada, Daniel Brooks, Elaine Marie Carnegie-Padgett, Ximena Escobar, & Shawn M. Klimek, Barrio Blues Press, 2020.

"The Final Gift," originally published in *Helios Quarterly Magazine: The Complete Series*, edited by Zelda Knight, Aurelia Leo, 2022.

Acknowledgments

Thanks to: Jendia Gammon and Gareth L. Powell of Stars and Sabers Publishing, for believing in this collection; Scarlett R. Algee for proofreading this book; Raul Cruz for the stunning cover; every person who took time to offer a blurb; my family and Chloe, who have all offered unwavering support. And to every publisher, editor, author, and reader who has taken a chance on me, guided me, believed in me, inspired me, or read my words, I love you all. Now and always.

About the Author

Pedro Iniguez is a horror and science fiction writer from Los Angeles, California. He is a Bram Stoker Award® winner, an Elgin Award nominee, a Rhysling Award finalist and a Best of the Net and Pushcart Prize nominee.

Apart from leading writing workshops and speaking at several colleges, he has also been a sensitivity reader and has ghostwritten for award-winning apps and online clients.

He is the author of *Mexicans on the Moon: Speculative Poetry from a Possible Future*, and the horror fiction collection *Fever Dreams of a Parasite*. His debut children's picture book, *The Fib*, is due out Fall 2025 from Gloo Books.